ARMISTICE
RUNNER

ALSO BY TOM PALMER

ARMISTICE
RUNNER

TOM PALMER

Conkers

First published in 2018 in Great Britain by
Barrington Stoke Ltd
18 Walker Street, Edinburgh, EH3 7LP

www.barringtonstoke.co.uk

Text © 2018 Tom Palmer
Illustrations © 2018 Tom Clohosy Cole

A CIP catalogue record for this book is available
from the British Library upon request

ISBN: 978-1-78112-825-1

Printed in Great Britain by Clays Ltd, Elcograf S.p.A.

This book is dedicated to all the volunteer coaches who give children the chance to enjoy running – with a big thank-you

ONE

Lily accelerated, keeping her eyes on the three girls ahead of her. She was ten metres behind them and within striking distance as they climbed the muddy, water-logged path.

Time to attack.

She pushed past the first of the three leaders, a thin girl in a white vest. Now Lily was in third place. Ahead of her were Gemma and Keeley. Older than Lily. Slower than Lily on the uphills. Chest hurting, legs hurting, everything hurting, Lily pushed herself hard.

She could hear her own lungs forcing air in and

out as she passed Gemma and Keeley. And, now she had taken the lead, she knew she had her breathing right.

The ground was firmer further up the hill. Not boggy like at the start of the path. But Lily placed her feet carefully, avoiding exposed roots and rocks that could mean a slip or a twist.

Attack.

Lily knew she had to keep at it, because now she could sense who was behind her. She couldn't see her, couldn't hear her, but she knew she was there all the same.

Abbie Granger. Arms pumping like an unhinged windmill, running on Lily's shoulder, waiting for her moment to overtake.

After pushing so hard up the hill, Lily was struggling to breathe evenly now. Beyond her comfort zone. She heard a voice in her head as she stared across the high open moor to the other side of the valley.

It's only a training run, the voice said. *Save your best for the big race.*

It was true, Lily thought. This, after all, *was* only a training run. The last training run before the first big fell race of the season. One that Lily would be racing. And one that Abbie would race too. In the Lake District village where Lily's gran and granddad lived. *That* was the important run, not this one.

Lily felt a crosswind ripple over the surface of the moor. The ground beneath her feet changed again to soft wet wild grass, damp working its way into her fell shoes.

Lily hated wind like this. It interfered with her breathing, breaking the rhythm of her ins and outs. She gazed beyond the top of the moor towards the range of higher hills in the west. Clouds drifted eastwards. Greys and whites. Like giant sheep grazing on the hills. Eyes back on the track, Lily saw some of the parents standing on the side of the course, Abbie's dad among them.

That was the moment that Abbie chose to make her move. She put on an explosion of pace where the track widened before it fell downhill, overtaking Lily.

Lily felt a burst of sudden sullen fury. What had she been doing staring at the clouds, thinking they looked like giant sheep?

Stupid.

Now she could hear Abbie's dad yelling at his daughter.

"Take her," he yelled. "Get her! Put her out of the race."

His words came as a shock to Lily, although Abbie's dad was always like that, always shouting at his daughter. OK, Abbie was in the lead now, but it wasn't even a proper race!

Faster. Harder. Lily felt the rhythm of her breath falter even more as she tried to match Abbie's speed. She wanted to reach out and grab her rival, pull her back. But Abbie was leaving her for dead now.

Lily wanted to cry out in anger. And she would have, if she'd been alone or somewhere Abbie couldn't hear her. Instead, she felt herself slow down, her head drop, a scowl numbing her face.

Downhill. Downhill all the way. Gemma and Keeley eased past her. Lily made up post-run excuses in her head.

My knee was aching.

I've got a cold coming on.

I didn't get to bed until late last night.

But none of those things were true and she

wouldn't say them. She'd run badly. And she'd run badly because she took her mind off running. Then – unforgivably – she'd given up and let herself be beaten.

Those were the real reasons.

Lily ran past her coaches, then she saw her dad and brother Tim. Tim was holding his hand up to make an L shape, mouthing *loser*. And Lily's head filled with thoughts. Bad thoughts.

She thought about the long drive to her grandparents with her idiot brother next to her on the back seat. About Abbie Granger and the race in a couple of days. About Gran being ill. And how it might be serious because she'd overheard Mum and Dad talking about it the night before.

The next three days might be hard.

TWO

The long drive to Gran and Granddad's was hard going. Motorways. Roadworks. Traffic jams. Lily, slumped in the back seat, replayed the last stages of the run against Abbie Granger. If only she'd gone faster up the hill. If only she'd not felt so deflated that she couldn't fight back when her rival overtook her.

What Lily really wanted to do was fill in her running log – the special notebook she kept every day. It was in the front pocket of her backpack, right there at her feet. But she couldn't do that in front of her brother. He would try to read it, then be deliberately annoying. And, to be honest, Lily wasn't sure how to write about the run yet.

Lily looked up to catch her mum's eye in the driver's mirror. Their eyes met for a second before Lily looked away.

"How are you feeling now, love?" Mum asked.

"Fine," Lily answered.

"Not," Tim scoffed.

Lily scowled at her brother.

"She's still cross about how that Abbie ran past her and beat her. Again," Tim said, leaning towards his sister. "And how those other two girls overtook her too because she gave up, and she's thinking about it because she lost and she hates losing, and now she's worried about the race coming up and ..."

Lily reached out and pushed her brother away. It made her mad that he knew exactly what she was thinking, exactly how she was hurting. How did he do that? He was just a stupid little boy, not a mind-reader.

"Oww!" Tim screamed, massively over-reacting. "Lily hit me, Dad. Lily hit me."

Dad snapped awake, then turned around.

"What happened?" Dad asked, his eyes red and puffy.

"I didn't hit him," Lily said. "I pushed him. Not hard. Just away."

"Well, just leave him, Lily." Dad sighed.

"Yes, Dad." Lily felt a ripple of anxiety pass through her. She needed to make life easy for her dad. He was worried about Gran.

"I wish I had a film of it," Tim sniggered. "If you let me have a proper phone, then I could have filmed it."

Dad's hand came over from the front seat and rested firmly on Tim's arm.

"You," he growled, "need to be nice to your sister. You need to be kind to her. Because at four o'clock we'll be at Gran and Granddad's. And we need to show that we are a nice happy family. Because Gran is not well and Granddad needs us to be calm and to help him. Understand?"

"Yes, Dad." Tim grinned a sarcastic grin. "I'm really happy. And I'm nice too."

"And you," Dad said. "You, Lily, have to snap out of this. You could win that race on Saturday. Or Abbie could. You need to prepare well and do your best. That's all you can do."

Lily looked into her dad's bloodshot eyes. "I know all that," she said, thinking about why his eyes might be so red.

"Good."

"But ..." Lily went on.

"But what?" Dad asked.

Lily wanted to ask about her gran. That feeling of panic was back. Had Dad been crying? Was Gran that bad? What was it going to be like? What if her gran didn't recognise her? It had happened to a girl in her class – she'd visited her granddad on his birthday and he'd not had a clue who she was.

"Nothing, Dad," Lily said.

Lily watched her dad nod, then take his hand off Tim's arm.

Silence.

Just the noise of a car moving past them in the outside lane. They were off the motorway now, moving along a dual carriageway that swept upwards around a wide hill.

Lily tried to think about the lake you could see from her gran and granddad's front garden, the white steamer that travelled up and down it during the summer. She thought about the rope swing by the water's edge. And the ice-cream shop. And the morning sounds that came through the open windows. Sheep baaing. Birds screeching and singing. And, best of all, the dogs. Lily loved her grandparents' dogs, Meg and Gus.

In the front of the car, Mum and Dad were talking. About how Gran's Alzheimer's was making it almost impossible for Granddad to cope. There was a catch in Dad's voice. He couldn't quite finish any sentence he started.

"Who's Al Zimers?" Tim interrupted. "Is he coming too? Is he American?"

Lily heard her dad laugh. "Alzheimer's," he said more clearly. "It's a disease that your gran suffers from. It means she forgets things. She might not remember who we are, Tim. You have to be ready for that."

Tim went quiet for a second, then said in a

cross voice, "Well, I might not remember who she is, then."

Lily stared out at the grasslands. Dry-stone walls cut the hillside into a patchwork of fields. And then – at a certain height – the vegetation changed colour. It turned brown and purple in patches. There were no more walls up there. Just scattered rocks and boulders. And the vast hills of the Lake District. Lily could see some sheep walking in a long dotted line up a track.

It was true that Gran was not like she used to be. Lily had always been so close to her, but now it felt like there was a thick pane of glass between them when they met. Lily shivered. What if Gran didn't remember *her*?

THREE

As soon as she walked into her grandparents' house, Lily understood.

Things had changed.

There were two bin bags in the hall, full of rubbish and tied at the top. The house smelled funny, not like its usual comfortable smell of Gran's home-cooked dinners or furniture polished until it gleamed.

Granddad had his arms open wide in welcome, but his eyes looked weary to Lily. His skin was grey and crumpled. Lily felt pain rising from her stomach to her chest. She clutched the present of a wrapped red scarf that she'd bought for her gran tighter in front of her.

"What's that weird smell?" Tim asked.

"I've let the place go, Timmy." Granddad tried to smile. "Need to concentrate on your gran. I keep the front room, kitchen and bedroom nice. The rest will have to go to the dogs."

"What have you done to Meg and Gus?" Tim asked.

"Tim," Mum rebuked.

"It's OK." Granddad sighed. "Tim can ask what he wants. There's no point avoiding the truth." Granddad looked at Lily as he replied in a softer voice. "The dogs live in the back garden now. In the shed. Keeps them out of our way."

The dogs lived outside! Lily had to stop herself gasping. She couldn't believe it. All the time she'd been growing up, Meg and Gus had been in the house. She loved them and they loved her. They felt almost like cousins to her, rather than animals. But now they were outside. In the cold.

"Come on in," Granddad said.

Gran was in the front room. There was a fire burning in the hearth, a neat stack of tinder and logs next to it, and a painting of hills on the wall above the fireplace. Lily smiled. Granddad was right. This room felt good. This room hadn't changed.

But Gran had. She looked smaller somehow. Lily hesitated for a half-second before going to give her a big hug. Tim stayed by the door and put his hand into his mum's.

They sat down in a circle of chairs and sofas.

Dad tried to start a conversation with his mum. But she seemed to be half dreaming, miles away. After a few attempts, Dad stood up, rubbed his face and left the room.

Lily gave Gran her present. Gran smiled when she saw the red scarf but put it aside without a word.

Then they had a bowl of soup together in the kitchen. Gran stayed in the front room, a sandwich on her knee. She didn't touch it.

Later, in the evening, they all sat together again. Granddad, his face flushed, had a bottle of beer and a glass in front of him. Lily sat with Gran, holding her hand. She still hadn't spoken. Granddad asked Lily and her brother what they'd been up to since he last saw them.

"Lily's been running," Dad announced.

Lily smiled. She didn't mind that her dad answered for her. She liked that he sounded proud of her.

"Another runner?" Gran said, her first words all day.

"She's a fell runner." Tim laughed. "It means she falls over a lot. Especially when Abbie is behind her."

"*Another* runner?" Dad asked, ignoring Tim. "What do you mean, Mum? I don't remember any other runners."

Lily felt her gran's hands close around hers.

"My granddad." Gran smiled. "Your great-great granddad, Lily. His name was Ernest. *He* ran the fells. Tell me about your running, Lily."

Lily could see that Mum, Dad and Granddad were on the edge of their seats, watching. Gran talking was a big deal. They smiled at Lily to encourage her to ask more.

So Lily sat with her gran. She talked about her running club. How they trained. And the two fell races she'd done last year. The old woman nodded as Lily spoke, but Lily didn't really want to talk about herself – she wanted to know more about her great-great granddad.

"Will you tell me about your granddad now?"

Lily asked, remembering how her mum had told her to encourage her gran to talk about her past. She looked at her dad and saw he was watching closely.

"He was a champion," Gran said, the pride clear in her voice.

Lily leaned forward. "Really?"

"Really," her gran said. "He won lots of races. It was before the war that he did his most famous run. He broke the record in the fell race here." Lily felt her gran's hand grip tight again. "And that record still stands. One hundred years later."

Lily loved the strength of her gran's memories of her granddad. She loved it that she had her fell running in common with a man, a part of her family, who'd lived a century ago.

"Which war?" Lily asked.

"The Great War, they called it," her gran said. "The first."

Lily remembered what she'd learned at school about the First World War. The trenches. The mud. The endless fighting that left millions of men dead.

"But Ernest never ran again after the war," Gran went on. "He came home safe, but my mum told me that he never ran again. He wasn't injured, but he put his running shoes in his box and closed it and that was it. Fit as a fiddle he was too."

Then Gran was on her feet, leaning on Lily to push herself up.

"Mum?" Dad asked. "Where are you going?"

"I have to go," Gran said, her voice wobbly with distress.

"No, Mum," Dad said. "We're staying here today."

"I have to go," Gran said. "Home."

Lily felt herself go cold all over.

Dad put his hand under Gran's arm. "*This* is your home."

"No." Gran pushed his hand away.

"Mum. Please," Dad said.

Lily felt sick. What had she done to make her gran like this?

"I'm not upset," Gran insisted, as if she'd been reading Lily's mind. "I need to get something for the girl." She screwed up her face. "For Lily. I need to find Ernest's box."

"Ernest's dead," Dad said.

"Oh, I know my grandfather's dead, silly boy," Gran snapped, as fierce as Lily had ever seen her. "He died on 31 July 1967 and we buried him a week later in the graveyard at Hawkshead. But I still have his box. If this is my house, then take me up to the loft. No one's looked at his things for years. Decades. Inside that box there's his running boots and log books. His vest, his race numbers. And his medals. I kept them all. I knew one day there'd be another runner in our family. I want to give the box to Lily. Ernest would have liked that."

Lily felt a burst of excitement as she understood she'd not upset her gran at all. It was the opposite, in fact. She'd made her happy. And now Lily was desperate to see what was in the box.

FOUR

Dad placed a wooden box on the coffee table in front of Gran.

Gran studied it, a smile lighting up her face. She ran her hands along the rough pale wood of the box, then touched the metal hinges and catch that held the lid in place. On one side **THREE CARTRIDGES FOR MORTARS** was stencilled in faded black letters.

"My granddad brought this box back from the war." Gran broke the silence in the room. "My mother told me that once he was home, he put his running kit inside the box."

"And never ran again?" Lily asked.

Gran shook her head. "Never. He gave it up for good. He would get the boots out and polish them with dubbin to keep them supple. He'd do it in spring when he saw the sun hitting the tracks he used to run. He lived here, you know. In this house. He'd polish them, then put them back in the box."

"So, he wasn't injured in the war?" Lily asked.

"No," Gran replied. "He was the fittest man I knew. Right up until he died. He'd walk and garden and row his boat. He farmed on the fells for a while between the wars."

Silence in the room. Lily didn't know what to say.

Gran came to her rescue and answered the questions Lily didn't know how to ask.

"He never explained why he stopped running," she said. "We always thought it was to do with the war, but the men who came home never spoke about what happened to them. And no one ever asked them."

Lily understood. She remembered how she'd cried when she'd done her homework on the First World War, when they'd held a Remembrance service at school. Maybe silence was the proper response.

"Open the box, Lily," Gran said. "See what's inside."

The catch was stiff, but after a few seconds Lily was able to unfasten it. As she opened the lid, Lily watched an explosion of tiny dust motes burst out of the box and sparkle in a shaft of sunlight coming in the window.

Lily blinked and looked inside. On the top there was a pair of light leather boots. They were like nothing she'd seen before, made of old cracked leather, brown. The laces were frayed, hanging limp. Lily lifted one of the shoes from the box and turned it over. Metal studs were driven into its sole.

She heard her gran breathe in, saw her smile. "Smell that," she said. "Dubbin. That's what he used to rub into them to keep them soft. He loved those boots. I always thought they looked like a weapon he'd use in the trenches more than they looked like shoes. Imagine getting hit with one of those."

Lily glanced at her dad. He was nodding at her. Lily took it to mean that she should empty the box. Everyone understood that to see and smell its contents was helping Gran to remember.

Next Lily took out a white T-shirt, its thin cotton stained and worn. Lily held it up so that everyone else could see it.

"Mud." Lily's mum grinned. "He must have been like you, Lily. Always covered in mud."

Then there were some clippings from old newspapers. Smudged black-and-white photos of crowds standing at the foot of hills. All in hats and long coats. Race numbers printed on squares of crumpled paper.

"People would come from miles around," Gran said. "A day out to watch the fell runners. They'd bet hundreds of pounds on who would win."

Underneath the newspaper clippings was a pile of notebooks bound together by two long shoelaces. Also, a small velvet bag that made a metal clinking sound when Lily lifted it from the box.

"Open that," Gran said. "I've not seen these for years. For more than years."

"Is it medals?" Lily's dad asked.

Lily looked up. Everyone was gathered round the table now, wanting to see what was inside the velvet bag. Their bodies blocked out the light from the window.

Lily did what she was told and untied the cord, with a glance over at the stack of notebooks she'd set aside. They all had black leather covers, fraying and cracked like the running shoes. Lily had seen the words *Running Log* scratched into the cover of the first one.

Her great-great granddad's running logs! He'd written a running log just like she did. But Lily would have to come to those later. First, she had to focus on the medals.

Lily's mum leaned forward and put a cushion on the table.

"Tip them onto there," she suggested.

Again, Lily did as she was told. Three medals fell onto the cushion. Two were attached to dull-coloured ribbons that could be hung around a person's neck. The other was larger and had a wider, shorter ribbon. It would be stuck with a pin to a soldier's uniform.

Gran pulled herself forward. "The big medal,"

she whispered, "was for going to fight in the Great War. All the soldiers got one. The other two are for running. One of them – I'm not sure which – is for winning the village fell race. That was in 1918. Before he went to France to fight."

There was another long silence as everyone studied the medals. Tim was asked to be careful and Lily was pleased he seemed to understand that they were precious.

*

Later that evening, Mum, Dad and Granddad sat in the kitchen with Tim and looked the medals up on Google.

Lily was alone with Gran, who had leaned back into the sofa and was smiling sleepily.

"Gran?" Lily said.

"Yes, love?"

"Please can I read your granddad's running logs?"

"You can." Gran smiled. "They're yours now, love. I want you to have all my grandfather Ernest's running things. You're the first runner in the family since him. So they should go to you."

Lily clenched her jaw to stop herself crying as she pulled at the string that bound the thick black notebooks together. Maybe her gran was OK after all. Her memories of her granddad were so clear. And she seemed content, not at all distressed like she'd been earlier that day.

The string round the log books fell away and Lily lifted the top notebook, turning it over in her hands. It was narrower than her school exercise books but with many more pages, printed with fine blue and red lines. She opened it and was hit by the warm, musty smell of old paper.

She saw some little drawings of routes across hillsides, in and out of valleys, then some numbers laid out in a chart. There were times and distances, neat notes about the weather. Even lists of what he'd eaten and how long he'd slept for. Lots of it was just like what Lily did in her own notebooks but the level of detail was fantastic.

Lily lifted the books and took the bottom one out. She opened it, aware that her brother was standing in the doorway, his eyes fixed on her in a bored way. She leafed through the book and what she saw surprised her. No more times and distances and diagrams. No more lists of meals eaten. Just words. Page after page of words in upright looping handwriting.

After flicking to a random page, Lily read:

I ran like the blazes back to my company. I

abandoned all my usual care and – for the first time out there in France – it felt like a real run, a fell race even. I gave it everything, full-lunged, feeling the pain pouring into my legs, because I was desperate to tell Captain Whitaker the news. I knew he was teetering on the brink, which meant that another week of this damn war and his nerves would be shredded, but this news would set him on the road to recovery.

Out there, in the abandoned fields and trenches, I could tell that most men knew the war was over. The Armistice had been signed. There was no relentless barrage now and the skies, which had thronged with planes all autumn, were empty and quiet.

What was this? Lily wondered. It seemed to be some kind of diary rather than a running log.

She looked at Gran, asleep now. Then she glanced over to Tim. His expression had changed from dull boredom to a flicker of interest. And if he was interested, he might spoil this for her.

"Shall we take the dogs out?" Lily asked.

Her brother grinned a yes. Lily packed the notebooks up and shut the lid on them. She was desperate to read them, but it was better this way.

FIVE

Lily and Tim walked the dogs down the hill, over the main road, then towards the lake. A walk to the lake was usually the first thing they did as soon as they arrived at their grandparents' house.

The edge of the water. It was like a ritual.

But today they had not come to the lake first, Lily reflected.

"It's dark," Tim said.

And it *was* dark. They couldn't see the lake or the mountains. Quiet too. No cars, no planes, nothing. Just the sound of the water lapping against the shore of the lake.

Tim insisted on holding both dogs' leads for the walk. He struggled as Meg and Gus pulled, excited to leave the back garden for the first time in a week. With her brother and the dogs occupied, Lily had time to think. To go over what had happened since they arrived.

Lily heard a sheep *baa* somewhere on the hillside, then the *baa* of another in reply. She loved these sounds of the water, the sheep, the Lake District at night. She'd grown up with them and they felt like a massive part of her life. One of the best parts. Now she realised that wouldn't always be the case.

Lily stared up at the sky. It was as black as the hills around them. The only difference between land and sky was that the sky was pinpricked with the pulse of tiny stars.

Lily was thinking about her gran. How she'd

barely spoken when they first arrived. Then, when the subject of fell running came up, how she'd become like the old Gran again. Lily felt proud about that. That she'd been the one who'd helped make Gran herself again.

Lily was excited, too, that Ernest's notebooks were more than just running logs. She felt like that rough wooden box held secrets. That it would offer answers to the question of why he had never run again.

She heard her brother mutter something but she ignored him. She wanted to think.

"Lily?"

Lily felt Tim's hand pulling at the sleeve of her coat.

"What?" she snapped, glaring at her brother only to see that his face was running with tears.

"I said is Gran going to die?" he said.

Lily stopped. She'd had no idea that her annoying little brother was thinking thoughts like that. Thoughts like hers. She pulled a packet of tissues out of her coat and dabbed her brother's wet face.

"No, Tim. She's just forgetful. She's not going to die." Lily tried to reassure him.

"But she's different," Tim said.

"She's got Alzheimer's." Lily swallowed. "It means she forgets. Her brain doesn't work properly. That's all."

"But why does she seem smaller?" Tim asked.

"I don't—"

"And why is she cross with Dad?"

"She—"

"And why do the dogs live outside? And why is Granddad sad? And why does the house smell funny?"

38

Lily didn't know what to say. She wished her mum or dad were there. They would take over. But she knew Tim wanted *her* answers, not theirs, even though she had none. So she pulled her brother to her in a big hug. His sturdy little body went limp in her arms. Lily felt the dogs nosing their way into the hug too.

"It tickles," Tim shouted. "Meg's tickling me."

And then Tim was laughing and tickling the dogs as they barked and jumped around them. Lily brushed the tears from her eyes and joined in with her brother's laughter.

SIX

Lily wanted to read Ernest's running logs. But first Tim had to go to sleep. Only then could she start. She had a plan – first, the walk. Now, a book.

Tim loved to be read to. And so Lily read her brother page after page of *Beast Quest* until he was asleep. She knew that once Tim was asleep, he was asleep for the night. Nothing would wake him.

It was nine-thirty when Lily picked up the first of her great-great granddad's log books and opened it at the first page.

17 April 1918

Large bowl of porridge

One apple

One pint of water

I ran from the village, up past the mines onto the fell. It was slow and steady going at the bottom, but I cranked up the pace where the track gets steep. I can run like the wind across even ground, but in these parts there's not much in the way of even ground. I need to ascend and descend faster.

I came down a faster route too, following the beck, not the track. Building up downhill speed and taking risks. The beck is great for that because the footfall is so uneven and slippery too. You said I needed to take more risks. You said I was too careful, too measured in my running, Fred.

Lily paused.

Fred?

Who was Fred?

The log book went on.

Thighs heavy and aching this evening. Walked it off around the village.

So, don't worry, Fred. I'm training. Doing what you made me promise to do. I'm rubbing dubbin into my boots once they're dry, to keep the toes soft, like you said.

And I'm keeping a running log for you to read when you get home. I don't know what else to write, Fred, other than my training and my food. But this is what you asked me to do, so I'm doing it.

I made a promise, so I'll stick to it. That was the deal. And I will stick to it, Fred. We've always made promises to each other and we've never broken them.

I promised to write this log book. I promised to run the village race on 1 June. And I promised to win it. This race has been run in the village for decades. If any one day is about our village and the people who live in it, this is it.

Before you went, you reckoned you'd be training in England for weeks before you got sent to France. And I'm reckoning the war will be over by the time you get yourself trained.

But now you've been away for a day. Just one day. It took hours to get back from the station after I came to see you off. The train pulled away and I set off on the walk home. But that breakfast Mother cooked for us kept me going. Black pudding and eggs. She made it special for you. A hero's breakfast, she called it. But I hope you don't have to be a hero.

The diary entry stopped there.

Lily frowned. There was a sketch of a hill. A cluster of buildings at the bottom, then a mountainside and a dark line inked onto the page. Ernest's route.

After that, these notes went on for a few more days. Comments on what Ernest had eaten, where he'd run and how he'd run. Things connected to his training that he wasn't satisfied with, ideas about how he could improve.

But then Lily noticed a change.

30 April 1918

Large bowl of porridge

Two apples

Easy lap of the lake this morning. I ran in the shallows at the edge of the lake for a while, choosing the right lines to keep the run as short as possible, following your advice – just so you know, Fred. Which meant I ran ten miles in eighty-five minutes.

As I ran, I thought about the war reports I had read in Dad's newspaper – about the U-boats, the German submarines, and how they had torpedoed a passenger ship in the Atlantic. Not even a ship with soldiers on. Hundreds of people drowned.

We need to stop the Germans, Fred, and I'm glad it's not long now until I can sign up and take my place at the front like you. I've been doing my bit here anyway. The Scouts have arranged for some of us to watch for German airships and aeroplanes. Remember our dream – to see a plane fly overhead? We used to draw them flying over the village. Well, the government have warned that the enemy might invade by landing on the lakes, or tarns, on the tops. Father says it's fanciful nonsense. But I climbed up to the tops and watched. So far, Father is right. I've seen no aeroplanes.

Other than that, I've been helping out on the farms – Jackson's and Wheelwright's. Their sons have gone to war, like you.

Anyway, Fred, I ran back into the village today to see a crowd outside Todd's, the butcher's. Mother had asked me to go on the way home. She'd given me a list of twelve items she needed from Todd's, Grim the grocer's and the hardware store.

"Don't forget any of them," she said.

"When does he ever forget anything?" Father said. "You could give Ernest a list of a hundred things to buy, send him up all the fells in Cumbria and he'd still not forget."

One of your rugby mates was standing at the butcher's. James Mawson, with a cluster of people around him. His younger brother, Billy, was there too, staring at the ground. When James saw me coming, he pulled away from the crowd and limped over.

"Ernest. I've a message for your mother and father," James said. "Can you pass it on?"

I nodded. "Of course."

"Fred's battalion. It's gone to France. They sailed on Tuesday."

"To fight?" I asked, sounding stupid. Like you might have gone for a day trip to France.

James gave me one of his gentle smiles. "He'll be all right, Ernest," he said. "Best prop in Cumbria, your Fred. Stop the Germans with a single shove of those shoulders of his."

I smiled back at him, but we also shared an uneasy glance.

"Will you tell your mother and father, then?" James asked. "He'll send a letter soon enough, I expect."

"I will. Thanks, James. How's the leg?"

James cursed. "I should be there with them," he said.

He's cut up about it, Fred. I could tell that he feels he's letting the village down. Letting you down. But he'd be useless out there with a dodgy leg. Shouldn't have dived into that muddy maul, should he?

After I'd done the errands, I went home and told Mother and Father about you. We ate in silence. Mother went to bed straight after and Father went out walking on the fells in the dark.

Lily looked up from Ernest's words.

She had that feeling she got when she read a story where someone goes off to war and everyone is worried. Then the people at home get some more bad news. Then there's a bit of good news. Then some really bad news.

But Lily reminded herself that this wasn't a story. This was a diary. It was real, not a story created to play with her emotions. In her history books, she'd read that about one in ten of the men who went to fight in the First World War had died. So, the chances were that Ernest's brother had come home.

But she wanted to know for sure. She looked at her watch. Ten forty-five. Late, but she had to read on. She had to find the answers to her questions.

Lily skimmed the rest of the first notebook. There was no more talk of war. Just running times, food, sketches of hillsides, pictures of exercises he'd done to strengthen his body. It was as if the war was over and the only thing Ernest had to worry about was his running.

Then everything changed.

SEVEN

31 May 1918

Porridge

Apple

Water

I left home just as the sun was coming up. I wanted to do a recce and check out the route for tomorrow's race. I knew which way I was going up. But I needed to make a few changes to the descent. There's that eight-foot drop onto sheer rock. It's risky, but it can save you the two hundred yards going round the back. I laid a thick layer of bracken over the rock so

I'd land softly. And there's that wall you hit on the final stretch, where the stones are wobbly. I found a part that was steady and packed in a couple more flat stones. That made it solid, so I knew I could hit it at speed, vault over and gain a few more yards again. Then I practised. Over and over.

While I was up there, I spotted a thin man dressed in rough clothes and with a filthy face. He was watching me through a gap in the walls. I recognised him. You remember Frank Thwaite? He was in the year above you at school and vanished when the first wave of men was conscripted. Everyone tells themselves he's away at war. Even his parents. But I know he's not, Fred. When I saw him, I thought, should I tell on him? Why should he get away with not doing his bit?

Then I remembered something you said to me once. If someone is troubled, be the first to comfort them. Then you can be proud of yourself. *So I went looking for Frank. To see if he was all right. I think you would have told me to do that. But he was gone. Hiding. Or maybe I'd not seen him, maybe my mind was playing tricks on me.*

Anyway, I soon forgot about Frank Thwaite. When I came off the hills, the village was deserted. The streets were empty of people and of delivery vehicles. The only thing that moved was the bunting for tomorrow's fell race.

I sprinted up the hill, trying to catch a glimpse of our cottage. I saw the front door was shut, and in that moment I realised all the front doors in the village were shut. And that was strange. Doors are always open in our village.

I knew then, Fred.

I ran flat out along the lane, opened the back door. There was no fire in the kitchen hearth, but I

could hear Mother's voice soft in the front room. And
another sound, a horrible animal sound of choking,
snorting, sobbing. I went into the front room and
Mother sat, staring back at me, Father's head in her
lap. It was him sobbing, not her.

On the floor was a piece of printed paper,
blanks filled in with blue handwriting.

A letter.

And I knew that it was about you, Fred.

Lily leaned back against the headboard, tears
streaming down her cheeks. Fred had been killed.
He was clearly dead. She looked at Tim and wanted
nothing more than to hug him.

Imagine. Her little brother – dead.

No. However annoying he was, Lily felt sick
at the thought of anything happening to Tim. She
climbed out of bed and went over to his, slipped her

arm under him, then put her head against his chest and squeezed.

When was the last time she'd done this? Hugged her brother? Twice in one day? When was the last time he'd let her? He was always so hostile now. He hated hugs. Hated shows of affection. But now she could feel the steady warmth of his breath. Lily smiled and eased away from him.

As she climbed back into bed, she lifted Ernest's notebook up to read some more. A sheet of paper fell out and floated to the floor. It was the thinnest paper Lily had ever seen. Delicate, almost transparent, and faded too.

FRANCE

30 MAY 1918

Madam

It is my painful duty to inform you that a report has been received from the War Office notifying the death of:—

(No.) _50337_ (Rank) _Pte_

(Name) _Frederick Darby_

(Regiment) _Border_

which occurred _whilst on duty on the front line_

on the _24th May 1918_

The report is to the effect that he _was_

killed in action

By His Majesty's command I am to forward the enclosed message of sympathy ...

Lily breathed out and looked at her watch. Ten to midnight. Late. But that didn't **matter**. She couldn't stop reading now.

This was about her family. About what had happened in this house.

Lily needed to know more.

EIGHT

1 June 1918

No porridge

No run

No strength exercises

Just darkness

With morning, light. Your bed, my bed, your coat hanging on the back of the door, your trunk with the picture of the cat you burned onto it when you were fifteen and Father went mad at you. I looked at all that and I wished it was dark again.

I lay there listening out for Mother and Father.

The house felt as good as dead. It felt like the whole village was dead. You aren't the only one killed, Fred. There are others. Samuel Halton is dead. Arthur Dalzell too. Both Cumbrian men and both fathers with five young kids between them.

We could have lain in our beds all day, all week, but then I thought again of what you said to me when I saw you off on the train.

"I might die," you said as the train started to blow off steam. "And if I do, it's up to you, Ernest, to give Mother and Father something to live for. I need you up on your feet. I need you to give them a purpose. To give them their bloody breakfast if it comes to it. Do you promise?"

"I promise. I'll do it. I promise you, Fred."

"You know that when you promise to do something, you have to do it. Do you understand that too, Ernest?"

0

"I do."

"I'll hold you to it. You break that promise and I'll haunt you."

"Haunt me," I begged now. "Haunt me."

But you didn't.

I got up and opened all the curtains in the house, then I stood by the front door, breathing in and out before I dared to open it. I walked down the hill to fetch milk, a loaf of bread, some bacon. It was Saturday, our bacon and egg day before the war and the only meat day during the war. Nothing was the same, but I thought it would be good if something was how it always had been.

As I walked down the hill, I saw that the lake was still. The sunlight so clear. The reflection coming off North Fell on the far shore of the water was like a painting. Perfect race conditions.

And then I realised it was race day.

The race. Every first Saturday in June is when it's run. It has been for years. But not today. Not with the news.

Further into the village and I saw that the race bunting was still out. A couple of lines strung across the road.

And then I saw Billy Mawson. Poor shy Billy. I bet he was dreading meeting me. He didn't know what to say. We stood there staring at the race bunting as it flapped pointlessly in the breeze.

Then Billy blurted it out. "I wish your kid was here. I wish he was warming you up and sending you up that hill." He paused. Then he said in a strangled voice, "I'm sorry, Ernest."

I shook his hand. But I didn't speak. I couldn't.

Then I noticed that over at the pub there was a cluster of men standing in front of the picket fence, one of them slumped down on a barrel, his feet dangling and kicking. They wore coats and hats, even though the day was already warm. As soon as they saw me, they straightened up. The one on the barrel jumped down and brushed off his coat.

And, Fred, I realised who they were.

Runners, here for the race. Runners from Keswick, Kendal, Windermere. Most of them were young ones, like me. But there were older ones too. Fell runners with grey hair and knotted sinewy legs. I realised they must have stayed overnight at the pub and that – by the look of them now – they wanted to get out of the village and leave us to our grief.

Then, among them, I saw old Joseph Grierson, telling them the race was off. And I had an idea. An idea that came from your voice in my head, reminding me of the promise I'd made you. To make Mother and Father proud, to give them something to live for.

I walked over to Joseph. The look on his face was pitiful, Fred. Desperate, like he was in a trap. He didn't know where to cast his eyes. Even old men like Joseph, men who've seen it all, don't know what to do in the face of this murderous war.

"Ernest." Joseph shook his head. "I'm sorry, son. I mean. To hear about your Fred. My God. I'm sorry. Please tell your father and mother … you know … I …" He couldn't go on.

"Thank you, Joseph," I said. "I'll tell them."

Joseph nodded.

"How's Mrs Grierson?" I asked.

Joseph shrugged. "She's well. But sad for your mother. And your father. Tell them if there's anything I can …" Joseph stopped, embarrassed and uncomfortable.

"I did want to ask you a favour, Joseph," I said.

"Anything, lad. Name it." Joseph looked like

he could weep with gratitude. I could see the relief in him that he could in fact do something, not just stand there all uneasy.

"I want you to hold the race," I said.

I saw the runners behind Joseph look up. Some were surprised. One or two shook their heads. Others were so eager for a race they couldn't hide it.

"Not today." Joseph looked at his feet. "Not after your Fred."

"Today more than any day," I challenged him. "Our Fred said I have to do ... I have to run it ... He told me before ..." That's when my voice broke.

"He's right, Joseph."

A woman's voice behind me. I swung round to see Mother. She'd come after me.

"Mrs Darby. I'm sorry ... I ..."

"Thank you," Mother said, taking my arm and standing with me. She was in her Sunday best. On a Saturday. Her good wool coat. Her shoes polished. And her hair up like she meant business.

"Our village has run this race for the last hundred years," Mother said. "It's always been run, and even though we've lost a dozen men from this valley they'd still want us to run. Our Fred told our Ernest to be sure to run it, so we'd better, hadn't we?"

I looked at her face. Her jaw was rigid and she was leaning her weight onto my arm. It took all my strength to hold her up.

"Yes, Mrs Darby," Joseph said, a briskness in his voice. "We'll run the race. Eleven o'clock start as scheduled?"

I walked with Mother up the hill. I might as well have been carrying her, the way she was leaning on me. She didn't say a word, but nor did I, and when we got into the kitchen, she started on the bacon straight away.

64

"Get you set for this race," she said. "Get you set to do what Fred told you."

"Yes, Mother."

"Did he tell you to win it, son?" she asked.

I nodded.

"You'd better do as you're told, then," she said, and she turned back to the bacon in the pan.

"Lily?"

A whisper across the bedroom. Lily's mum was in the doorway, squinting in at her.

"Hi," Lily said.

"Lights off." Mum frowned. "It's half-past midnight."

Lily sighed. Lights off? Now? She'd just found out that Fred had been killed and that Ernest was going to run in the race that very same day. And Mum wanted her to go to sleep?

Didn't she understand?

"Lily?" Mum said again.

No, of course she didn't understand. And Lily wasn't ready to tell her the story yet. She wanted to keep it to herself for a while.

Lily put the log book back on top of the others and smiled at her mum.

"Night, Mum. Sorry."

Her mum walked across the room, bent over the bed and hugged Lily.

"Night, Lily. Sweet dreams."

Then the light went out, leaving Lily in the dark, eyes open, a thought exploding in her mind. Was this the room where Ernest had lain that morning after he'd heard about his brother's death? The day he'd read that telegram from the War Office? Were his parents in the room next door, where Lily's mum and dad slept now?

Lily's mind raced with questions. Questions she hoped to find the answers to in the morning.

NINE

Lily woke the next morning to hear the noise of crockery and cutlery clinking from the kitchen beneath her bedroom. She peered over at Tim, then glanced at the box beside her bed. At the log books.

Tim fast asleep.

Log books to be read.

Lily was about to pick up the top one and carry on from where she'd left off last night, when she heard a cough from the kitchen. Gran's cough, but no other voices. Lily knew what that meant: her gran was up and nobody else was. Lily put the log books to the back of her mind, slipped a jumper over her pyjamas and went downstairs.

Gran was sitting in a dressing gown at the kitchen table, which was laid out with a jug of milk and a row of four unopened cereal boxes at the centre. There was a wipe-clean tablecloth on the table and a paper napkin at the side of each plate and bowl. A second jug sat full of orange juice.

"Been for a run, Lily?" Gran asked.

"Not yet, Gran," Lily said. "But I will later."

"Where are you going to run to? Up the fell?"

"Yes." Lily grinned, turning to look out of the window at the fell looming through the lace curtains. It was grey and craggy at the top. She felt her muscles twitch with the urge to run.

"I wish I could come with you," Gran said as Lily poured juice into two glasses. "I used to walk up there when I was younger. Your granddad and I could get to the top and back on an evening after he finished at the estate office. But ... oh, Lily, I'm so proud of your running. Are you going to win the race?"

Lily smiled and shook her head. "Probably not. I'm fast, but there's a girl called Abbie. She always beats me."

Gran smiled. "Is Abbie your friend?"

Lily shrugged, feeling Gran's gaze linger on her. "Not really," she said.

"Just your rival, then?"

"I suppose," Lily said. "She's quite competitive."

Gran paused. "That's good, isn't it?"

"Not for me." Lily tried to smile.

Gran picked up her glass of juice. She drank a little, then refilled it, right to the top.

"Abbie always beats me at the end of the race," Lily explained, wondering if this was the first time she'd put these feelings into words. "I stay ahead of her and then her dad starts shouting and she comes running through and beats me. I kind of give up when I feel her coming past me. And then she's often sick after. Sometimes she's sick before."

"Do you help her? I mean to say, when she's sick?" Gran asked.

Lily felt herself chewing the inside of her lip. "No," she said. "I would. But her dad keeps her away from the other runners. I sometimes talk to her at training. And sometimes her dad is, like, cross with her, so I talk to her then." Lily tried to smile. "I've got some other friends at running too. They're nice."

"Abbie's dad sounds like he's the problem," Gran said, turning her glass in her hand, spilling a bit onto the cloth. "Not Abbie."

"What do you mean?" Lily asked.

"Well, children are just children. It's their parents that make things difficult. Abbie's dad pushes her so hard it makes her sick. He sounds like a dreadful man."

Gran's hands twitched, her glass overturned and suddenly there was juice on the table, soaking into the boxes of cereal. Lily jumped up and grabbed a tea towel as Gran sat and watched.

Lily cleaned it up. After she'd finished, Gran smiled a thank-you and poured more juice into her glass.

"Are you going for a run today, Abbie?" Gran asked.

Lily stared at Gran. She felt a pain in her stomach. It was only a question. A repeated question. But it made her feel terrible that Gran had called her Abbie.

"I am," Lily said, trying to keep a smile on her face.

"Will you go up the fell?" Gran asked.

"I think so," Lily replied, panic rising up through

her chest into her throat. Then there was a long painful silence that bothered Lily so much she had to speak.

"I read Ernest's diaries," Lily said.

"Diaries?" Gran said. "His running logs, you mean."

"Yes, but they are more than running logs, Gran. He wrote them during the war. He writes about his brother, Fred."

Gran gasped. "Great Uncle Fred. He was a war hero. A rugby player too. My granddad had a photograph of the two of them together. On the fells. Both of them in hats and coats."

"That sounds like Ernest and Fred." Lily grinned, glad Gran was being Gran again.

"Is Fred coming to see us?" Gran asked.

"No, Gran." Lily shook her head. "He died."

Gran stood up. "Dead?"

Her chair fell backwards, clattering. Lily grabbed for her so she didn't fall too.

"In the war, Gran." Lily felt her heart pounding as if she was afraid.

"No." Gran shook her head, a sharp tone in her voice. "Who told you that?"

"It was in Ernest's diaries," Lily said, recoiling. She'd never heard such anger from her gran before.

"Silly girl. They're up on the fells. They'll be back soon."

Lily said nothing. She had no idea what the right thing to say was now. She wondered if there even was a right thing.

The silence was broken by footsteps coming quickly down the stairs. Dad was first through the door. Then Granddad.

Lily ran past them and upstairs, trying not to burst into tears till she reached her room.

TEN

Ten minutes later, Lily sat on the back step, lacing her fell shoes. She knew she should be having a rest day with the race tomorrow. But she also knew she had to get out of the house.

"Off for a run?" It was Dad.

"Yeah," Lily replied.

"Want me to come?" Dad asked.

"Can I go on my own, Dad? Please?"

Dad hesitated. "Sure," he said. "Everything OK, love?"

Lily nodded, then heard herself say, "Not really."

Dad sat down next to her. He was still in the

T-shirt and pyjama bottoms he wore for bed. His stubble caught in Lily's hair when he kissed the top of her head.

"What happened?" Dad asked.

"Gran spilled her juice," Lily said.

Dad didn't reply.

"She forgot my name," Lily whispered.

Dad sighed. "They're little things," he said.

"They're *big* things." Lily raised her voice. "She's not ..."

Dad put his hand on Lily's back. "Hear me out. What I wanted to say is that they might seem like little things taken on their own. But you're right to feel funny about them, because they're signs of a *big* problem. Your gran isn't who she was. And the little things are sometimes the hardest ..." Dad stopped speaking and stared up at the fell and the blue sky above it.

Lily stared with him.

"It's hard," Dad said.

Lily nodded. Then she had a horrible thought. That the same thing might happen to her dad one day.

She stood up. "I need to go for this run."

*

Lily pushed herself up the fell. She passed early-morning fell walkers. And sheep. Lots of sheep. The sun was up over the back of the fell now and she felt its warmth. She ran up the gentle sloped track towards the mines. Then the path got steeper. Over rougher ground, scree and rock jolted her feet and ankles. And that felt good. She liked the feeling of power over the terrain. She was glad of the strain in her legs and back. And the way her lungs hurt.

She pushed herself until she reached the top of a ridge.

Then harder still.

So hard she felt she couldn't go on. But she did. She wanted to see what would happen if she pushed and pushed. Faster, faster. Harder, harder. Until, eventually, her legs gave way. Like they had been swept from beneath her by a rock slide. She collapsed onto the rough path and gasped for air, her heart pounding.

It took her a couple of minutes to get her breathing right. She pulled out her water bottle, then drank from it, gazing down at the lake below. The thrill of after-running coursed through her. And the view thrilled her too. The lake, surrounded by its ring of mountains. The vast sky above. This view was the best thing in the world. But it didn't stop her mind from racing.

Gran. Gran was only going to get worse and there was nothing anyone could do.

The race. Would she lose to Abbie?

Abbie and her dad. Gran had made her feel sorry for Abbie, not hate her.

And then there were the log books. And Ernest. Ernest, who had sat right here on the ridge where she was now. Had he won his race? Did he go to war? Had he ever got over the death of his brother?

Lily stood up, ready to descend the fell and read some more of the diaries. She'd take it easy on the way down – no point injuring herself before the race.

When she got back to the house, everything was calm. Gran was in the front room with the TV on, although she was staring at the painting over the fireplace.

"She's not really talking," Mum said. "Why don't you have a nice long bath, Lily? Get your legs ready for tomorrow? Your dad's out with Granddad and Tim. They might be a while."

Lily nodded. She'd go upstairs. But have a quick shower, not a bath. Then read Ernest's diary. A while was good. She needed it. She needed to know more about what her great-great granddad did next. In the race. In the war.

ELEVEN

1 June 1918 (continued)

Eleven a.m. Joseph Grierson called the runners together and we gathered at the lake, ready for the start. You know how it works, Fred. The tradition that runners start from the edge of the lake, our shoes actually in the water. Then we run to the top of the fell, take a ribbon from Mrs Grierson and hurtle back to the water. Any route we like. Just up to the top and down again.

Except that today was different. There was no calling out from the crowd and no gambling. You'd have found it strange, Fred. There was barely any noise at all.

I studied the other twenty racers as they limbered up or stared at the mountain, the wooded slopes, then the bare rock and scree. There were two types of runner. Old runners like Jack Page and his brother Dan. Former champions. Then the young ones like me.

No one in between. All those other men away at war. Or gone.

"Ready, lads?" Joseph said.

We all bent low, our arms out at an angle. Get a good start, you always said, Fred. Get to the front. So I promised myself to be in first place by the time we reached the road.

"On your marks ..."

I heard one of the lads cough. Another slapped his thighs to force the blood into the muscles, ready

for the off. A third breathed fast and deep, getting
his lungs working.

"Go."

We were off.

I took it fast. Too fast. A sprint to get to the
front and not be caught up behind someone running
too slowly or stumbling. I had the lead by the time
we reached the road, like I'd planned. Then you said,
Not too fast, don't overdo it. And I felt like you were
alongside me, giving me advice, Fred.

I eased off as we raced, breathless, up the
village. The worst part is always the start, getting
the blood and oxygen to flow makes it worse than
the steepest of hills.

As soon as I slowed, two lads rushed past me. I'd
seen one of them before. Arthur Evans, from Patterdale.
And another with him. I was third as we left the
village. But by the time we were on the flat, I was fifth.

Arthur and his mate were fifty yards ahead. And you were saying, Push on, keep with them, don't give them too much of a lead. *But when we passed the mines, half way up, they pushed on. Not me. And I remembered what you said about choosing a line. Navigating. Using my head, not just my legs, to race. So I shaved off a few yards here and there by not following the path, by going over rocks, through streams. It worked. A little. But I was still losing ground.*

I'd say they had a hundred yards on me when I made my decision.

I decided to stop listening to you, Fred.

And there was only one way I was going to do that.

Pain.

I accelerated when we hit the foot of the steep. I tore past Jack Page and his brother. It hurt in my lungs and in my thighs, like a sprint gone on too long. But most of all it hurt in my head. And I knew that if it hurt, it was fast. And that if it hurt, I didn't have to listen to you or think about you.

But even with all that pain there was no catching Arthur and the wiry lad. They were a good eighty yards ahead when they crested the summit.

Just before I reached the top, and Mrs Grierson with her ribbons, Arthur and the wiry lad came down the other way. I saw their faces light up with the joy of descent. I had to step out of the path. They weren't giving ground. No chance. And why should they? They both had their eyes fixed a few feet ahead, watching for a safe place for their feet to fall. And that was fine, because I wasn't looking at their eyes either. I was looking at their feet to see how they were doing on the rock.

Steady and careful were the words I'd use for their downhill style. Perhaps they thought they didn't need to take risks because they had a hundred yards on me now. They had no need to be reckless.

But I could be reckless.

Still hurting, I pushed on. I took no break for a breath. Above me, rocks thrust themselves out of the fells. Everything looked raw, as if the glaciers that had formed these valleys had only last night passed through and ripped earth from stone.

I took my ribbon from Mrs Grierson. She gave me a sad smile and I tried to smile back, although it must have looked like a grimace as I struggled to catch my breath.

Then I attacked. I ran hard, letting my weight propel me down the hill, nearly twisting my right ankle before I was off the rock.

Hard, hard, hard down the hill.

Long jolting strides. My breath ragged and uneven.

It was the only way. You'd told me to win the race, so I had no choice. Every foot strike sent a sharp pain juddering up my calves, up my thighs and back. Every time I placed my foot, I risked injury. And there you were alongside me again. There was no getting away from you.

Fall down the hill. Relax, *you said.* You're trying too hard.

So I gave in to you and relaxed, let myself fall down the mountain. I did that thing I never do. I took the brakes off. I mastered that freedom you always said I had to if I was ever going to compete. And I took those two short cuts you'd set me up to do. I landed neatly on the bracken at the bottom of that eight-foot drop and I vaulted that wall without pausing. I was flying, Fred.

They had fifty yards on me by the time we reached the mines. I saw them look back once they were on the flat ground, then I ran harder still, so the lead was thirty yards as we came into the village. And the two leaders were split now. Arthur falling back, but the unknown young lad still striding on.

I overtook Arthur just before we reached the road.

We were both twenty yards behind the lad. Two hundred to run.

Arthur slowed down. He knew I had him.

"Go on, Ernest," he gasped. "Win it."

So I pushed on. The pain in my lungs burning. Over the road, fifteen yards behind. I could see the leader's silhouette against the lake, shimmering water reflecting sharp light back at me. It was so dazzling that when I noticed a man in a uniform standing at the side of the road, clapping, I thought it was you.

Do you remember when we were kids, Fred?

When Jack Page overtook his brother just short of the lake? The noise. There were five thousand watching. They were shouting, screaming, calling out. Most of them had a bet on Jack, not Dan. The noise as the two runners came in was like an avalanche coming down the mountain – or a storm at the far end of the valley.

There was nothing today.

Nothing as I closed in on the wiry lad and came level with him.

Nothing as I overtook him yards short of the lake.

Nothing as I hit the lake and fell into the dark water, gasping for breath, terrified of turning around to face anything so sickening as victory or congratulations. Or Mother. Or Father. Or that soldier clapping me. And most of all, not you, not facing you. Because you couldn't have been there.

So I waded deeper out into the water. My feet left the ground and I was swimming. Swimming hard to hold on to the blinding white heat of pain as the cold water seared into me.

TWELVE

1 June 1918 (continued)

Mother was waiting for me when I got home. She had a towel ready and a fire burning in the hearth. There was a medal on the table.

"Well done," she said. Only she said it in that way that leaves you wondering quite what she means. Was she saying well done for winning the medal? Or well done for jumping in the lake, making myself – and her – look like idiots?

After the race and after I'd gone in the water, I'd swum up the lake a bit and sat on the edge. On the rock under our rope swing. And I thought about how, even though I'd run the race, I hadn't got away from the pain.

I needed to keep running. I had this thing deep inside me. A hunger for revenge. They'd taken you, Fred, and I couldn't live with myself if I didn't do something about it. If I could do something, then I wouldn't feel as impossible about you. I needed an eye for an eye.

"Dry yourself, Ernest," Mother said.

"I want to go," I replied.

She glared at me, saying nothing.

"I want to go and fight," I said.

"I know you do," she muttered. "I'm your mother. I know what you're going to think next even before you do."

"Well, Mother, do I have your blessing?" I asked.

"No, you do not," she replied.

"Why not?"

"Because you can't." Mother folded her arms and stood with her back to the hearth.

"I can," I insisted. "I'm nearly old enough. I can join up now and tell them I'm eighteen. Lots of people have done it."

She shook her head.

"What does that mean?" I asked.

"Why would you want to go and do it?" She ignored my question.

"Why not?" I asked back. "I've told you. I look old enough."

She turned to check the kettle was coming to the boil, her back to me now. She put her hands against the lintel above the fire, leaning into the heat. I could see her breathing in and out, her apron string taut around her back, like she was a tethered animal.

Then, suddenly, she was facing me. "Where's Fred?"

"What?" I said.

"Where is he?" she repeated.

I didn't know what she was saying, but I did know I had to answer her straight.

"He's passed away," I said in a quiet voice.

"Passed away?" Mother shouted as the kettle screamed. "He's dead, Ernest. His body is lying in some filthy muddy field and I won't even get to bury him. He'll lie there without a grave. Without a funeral. Without God's blessing, even." She paused. "I have to live with that for the rest of my life, for every moment until I'm dead too. And the only thing stopping me being dead on the ground with Fred is you. My heart beats for both of you, Ernest. And I live for you. You're my only living son, and that's why you're not going to war."

What was I supposed to say to that, Fred?

Mother went to the range and lifted the kettle off the hob. She poured a little water in the teapot and swished it round, emptied it. Then she spooned tea leaves in and poured water on top of them.

"I can't live here any more," I said. I could hear myself crying, but I pressed on, shouting to stop my voice from faltering. "I can't walk round town, run on the hills, go to the mines, knowing that what I should be doing is fighting out there, doing what I'm meant to do. If I don't, I'm as good as dead."

Mother put the teapot down and faced me. Her expression was rigid. She eyed me and I eyed her back for what seemed like an hour.

"No," she said.

Windermere Station, 2 June 1918

I'm on the train. First Carlisle, then France.

I woke up early, long before Mother and Father. I knew what was going to happen this morning. Mother would get Father to join in telling me not to go to war. That I was their only son. That they needed me. That I was too young. And after all that I'd be stuck. They'd make me feel so guilty that I'd promise to stay.

And I've never broken a promise, Fred. I learned about promises from you.

So I made a promise to myself. I'd go to France. I'd fight. That was what I had to do now. A promise is a promise.

I packed what I needed and crept down the stairs. There was a faint smell of black pudding in the hallway. The memory of that smell of the breakfast Mother cooked the day you went off to war. Your hero's breakfast. And I decided I'd take that smell as a memory. Maybe she'd cook it for me when I got back. When the war was over. If she ever forgave me for walking out without her blessing.

I moved slowly, avoiding the three creaky steps like we used to when we went to raid the larder in the middle of the night, and I pushed the door carefully. I didn't want to wake them.

I stepped into the kitchen and saw Father first. He was sitting at the table with a cup of steaming tea in front of him. Next I smelled the black pudding. And eggs. And bacon. And fried bread. Then, finally, I saw Mother.

She didn't say anything.

She put my hero's breakfast in front of me.

Lily was stunned. That breakfast Ernest's mum had

made for him. Did it mean she had changed her mind overnight and that Ernest had gone to war? *With* her blessing?

She was desperate to know more. But not only about that. There was also what Ernest had said about getting revenge. That troubled Lily. She knew that on the field of war there was every chance he'd kill a German. But that whole eye-for-an-eye thing didn't feel right. Did he? Did he kill someone – for revenge? How would she feel about him then?

With so many questions in her head, Lily read on.

But the next diary entries were short. There was nothing about Ernest's argument with his mum or how he felt about his brother. Just short entries about training – army training. About being exhausted. About guns and bombs and trenches. Two or three lines every few days for eight long weeks.

Lily felt frustrated. What had happened to Ernest? Had he just stopped writing about his feelings, stopped writing to Fred now that he was at war too?

And then, at last, the diary changed again. Ernest had written a much longer entry. From France. Lily knew this was the start of a whole new chapter in Ernest's life.

THIRTEEN

English Channel, 1 August 1918

I'm on a ship, Fred.

We're crossing the English Channel. It's nothing like the lake at home. It's a strange world of grey. The dark sea, the patchy sky, even the ship – all grey. It's like the colours of the world have drained away as we approach war.

I'm a signed-up soldier with the British Army. We've done our training. I know how to dig a trench. I know how to aim a rifle at a German and fire. I know how to lob a Mills bomb into an enemy position.

I was worrying about the U-boats. But then one of the crew assured me that most of the German submarine force has been sunk, has broken down or is out of fuel.

We've shipped out to France earlier than we'd expected to, Fred. Just eight weeks of training, not ten. The men who've been out here before say there's something going on. Lots of companies heading out to France at once. Many more than usual. The kind of movement that happens when there's a big push on. They say we'll be in the reserves to back up the battalions on the front line to begin with. But I wish we were going straight up there, Fred. I'm keen to fight – keen to avenge your death.

Fred, there's an officer on the deck with me. He's keeping his distance, but he keeps on looking over. And when he does, he looks familiar, somehow.

Boulogne, France, 2 August 1918

So, that man last night on the boat, Fred. The officer on the deck. He came over to speak with me. You won't believe this.

"Private?" he said.

I stood up. Saluted. "Yes, sir."

I have to say, Fred, I was panicking. I was thinking, what have I done?

"I know you," he said.

"Sir?"

"Ernest Darby?" he asked.

"Yes, sir," I replied.

And then I heard in his voice a hint of Cumbria. A bit like those brothers we knew who went to Sedbergh School.

There was a break in our conversation at this point. An officer was leading his platoon on a march around the decks, barking at them as he did so.

"I want you fit as footballers when you come off this troop ship," he yelled. "I don't want you lying around smoking. We are going to be moving fast when we hit the ground. The enemy is on the run. You and the rest of the British Army are going to drive them back into Germany so that we never see their ugly German faces again. And that means I want you strong and ready to go. Five laps. Now."

"I'm sorry for being so mysterious," the first officer said to me once the other men had passed by. "I'm Captain Whitaker."

"Sir?" I still had no idea how he knew my name.

"I was at the village fell race. On leave, recovering at a hospital near Kendal." Captain Whitaker tapped his leg. "And I saw you come in." He smiled. "Then jump in the damn lake. That was one hell of a way to mark becoming a champion fell runner."

And then I knew him. The clapping soldier on the side of the road. I felt I owed him an explanation.

"It was the day after I heard my brother died, sir," I said. "Fred Darby. Private Fred Darby. Border Regiment. Did you know him?"

"I regret I didn't know your brother. And I am sorry to hear he was killed. In action, was it?" Captain Whitaker asked.

"Yes, sir. A shell," I told him.

"It can't have been easy running that day," Captain Whitaker said.

I shrugged. "To be honest, the news made it easier, sir."

Captain Whitaker let out a short laugh then. "I'm sorry, Private Darby," he said. "I laugh because I think I understand what you mean."

"Yes, sir."

I was sure he did understand. I had no doubt

he'd seen dozens of men die in France. He'd have had to fill in the forms to let the families know, like the form Mother and Father had been sent.

Captain Whitaker took a deep breath and stared out at the sea. Then he turned back to me. "You're Border Regiment too, I see, Private Darby."

"Yes, sir," I replied.

He nodded, then bit his lip. I noticed his eye twitching rapidly.

"I'm going back to the front straight away," he said. "And, Private Darby, you might be aware that the front is moving rapidly forward?"

"Yes, sir."

"Things are stretched out there, Private. I've heard that units are making as much as a mile in one day. And that creates problems. Communication, you understand," he mused. "We're moving so swiftly we aren't laying down wires. No telephones. And the radio is hopeless over distance. There's no reliable means of staying in touch with HQ."

"I understand, sir," I said.

"What we need – what I need," Captain Whitaker said, "is a runner."

"A runner, sir?"

"I need a man with me all the time. Someone I can give a message to and send him off back behind the lines to HQ, or across to the next company, left or right. It's vital. Otherwise men get stranded. Soldiers end up behind enemy lines. It's a nightmare. Do you have a good memory, Private?"

"I do, sir."

"Can you tell me what that officer said to his men just now? In as much detail as you can?" Captain Whitaker asked.

"Sir," I didn't hesitate. "He said he wants them to be as fit as footballers when they come off the ship.

He doesn't want them lying around smoking. He told
them that they are going to be moving fast when
they hit the ground. That the enemy is on the run.
That they and the rest of the British Army are going
to drive the enemy back into Germany so that we
never have to see their ugly German faces again. And
that means he wants them strong and ready to go.
He took them on five laps of the ship, sir."

"Good. Very good. I'll speak to your commanding
officer." Captain Whitaker smiled as he studied me,
his eyes burning into mine. But the left one still
twitched ceaselessly.

And it's funny, Fred. There I was going off to
fight the Germans and take my revenge for your
death, and now I'd been asked to run messages, not
fight at all.

Did I feel disappointed?

I'll be honest, Fred. I didn't. I felt proud. Proud

that a man like the Captain had asked me to do

something for the war effort that he thought I'd be

good at.

FOURTEEN

France, 5 August 1918

How do I describe the front line, Fred?

A million men lined up in a trench eight foot deep, facing another million men looking back the other way at them. This, over hundreds of miles across Europe.

Craters. Collapsed trenches. Rain. Cold. Mud. The stink of death. And the noise of shells coming in, like a dozen trains ripping through a station every few seconds.

I hardly need to describe it to you, do I?

Captain Whitaker took me with him to the front. He was desperate to join his men. We didn't stop moving from the minute we walked off the troop ship.

"Come on, Private Darby. I need to get back to my company."

All the time I did my best to try to adjust to the way the air was thumping with explosions and the way I could feel the earth shudder under my feet, as if there was some terrible ogre down there. I didn't want to trouble Captain Whitaker with my fears. And I didn't have time to take it all in at the start, I suppose. I was right next to Captain Whitaker, doing everything I could to be attentive, like a sheepdog at a shepherd's heels, waiting for his order. Not on the fire step. Not on sentry duty. Dull, in some ways. But at least I'm still alive.

So I kept myself busy. I studied maps of the

area, *to get to know the terrain better, aware we'd be moving out of the trenches soon. I went on short sorties alone, to assess the land, so that when the call came I would know where to go and how to get there as quickly and safely as I could. In some ways it was like doing a recce for a fell race.*

And then my first orders came.

"Come, Darby," Captain Whitaker said.

In Captain Whitaker's bunker, there was a map spread out on a table, lit by two oil lamps dangling from a beam in the roof. The Captain pointed at the map.

"We're here. Can you see that? West of this ridge."

"Yes, sir," I said.

"I've identified two enemy machine-gun nests out there. One on the ridge itself. The other to the side. HQ are not aware of them. If we push on when

the Germans retreat, those two machine guns will mow us down. I need you to go back to Battalion HQ and show them on their map where those nests are. They'll hit them with shells. Then we can advance. I want you back here before dawn. Understood?" he asked me.

"Yes, sir."

He pointed out the machine-gun nest positions. I scanned the map, memorised its lines and how they would translate out there on the ground.

"Don't take all your kit with you. Leave your entrenching tool. Take only fifty rounds. The rest should remain here. Make yourself a bit lighter. Understood?"

"Yes, sir."

"Something else," Captain Whitaker said. "You understand, don't you, that the Germans are desperate. If they catch you, they'll take you to their

HQ and they'll torture you to find out what we're planning. So don't get caught."

"I won't, sir."

"Better to be shot than caught," he warned me.

"I understand, sir," I said briskly, though his words chilled me. And then I was off.

I was mad keen to get it right. But it was hard. Hard and horrible to run in heavy clothes made heavier still by rain soaking into dirty wool and heavy boots.

First up, I ran through a line of old communication trenches. Most of them were crumbling and collapsing. So I felt it'd be better to run above ground.

I scrambled out. Big mistake.

At first I enjoyed being out there in the open. Running as well as I could while carrying all that kit. The ground was solid on the top. Easy to cover if you avoided the uneven craters and burned-out woods.

A mile short of HQ, I heard an engine noise. Not behind me. Not ahead of me. And I scanned around, confused, as the noise grew louder and louder, but still I saw nothing. I thought I'd gone mad, then I saw a line of puffs rising a little from the soil, tearing towards me. And the noise of incoming fire.

I flung myself down into a shell hole, landing on my back, face up to see a dark shape swoop out of the sky, then the smell of petrol, the rattle of gunfire, and a shape like that of a huge bird blocked out the sun for a second.

It was an aeroplane, Fred. A great big aeroplane.

And, Fred, I laughed. You know, like you, I'd always wanted to see an aeroplane fly and now I had, and it had come within inches of filling me with bullets.

I couldn't resist climbing out of the hole to see

the plane turn and head back the way it had come.
Into the sun, where it vanished.

Lily put the log book down. She had heard voices. And, for a minute, she was so gripped that she couldn't remember the time of day, what was going on in her life, whether it was summer or winter. Then it came back to her. Gran, Tim, Dad, Abbie. Her real, ordinary life away from the pages of Ernest's diary.

She realised Dad was back with Tim and Granddad, which meant Tim might come up at any moment and she'd have to stop mid-sentence.

Lily put the log book back in the box and went downstairs. She'd return to Ernest and his running amid trench warfare later. She needed to know he was safe, that nothing bad had happened to her great-great granddad or to Captain Whitaker.

FIFTEEN

"All ready for the race tomorrow, Lily?" Granddad asked at dinner time.

"Yes, thanks," Lily said. "I'll get an early night and a good sleep. Then I'll be fine."

"You will." Granddad smiled.

"I used to walk on the fells with my granddad," Gran said. "He took me up there and showed me an old sheep hut where a man used to live. Granddad told me he lived there all the years of the war. And nobody knew except him. He was hiding from the fighting."

Lily noticed the other adults sharing looks, as if

they didn't know if Gran's words were true or made up. She was desperate to say that it was true and to prove it – with the log books – but she was worried that she might upset Gran. It was best, she decided, to say nothing.

"I'd like to go for a walk on the fells now," Gran said.

"Maybe tomorrow, love," Granddad said. "It's getting dark and they've forecast rain."

"Hmmm," Gran said, and she directed her angry face at Granddad. Lily could tell she wanted to go, never mind the dark or the rain.

An uneasy silence settled over them all. Lily frowned. All her life, she'd assumed adults knew exactly what to say and do in any situation. Now she knew better.

"If it rains, it'll be wet on the fells," Lily said cheerily, trying to break the mood.

"Is that a problem?" Granddad asked.

"I like it when it's muddy. I've got decent fell shoes – they grip properly. The mud doesn't slow me down like it does some of the others."

Gran put her hand on Lily's. "Help me up please, love," she said.

Lily stood up and Gran levered herself up. She could see that Granddad, Dad and Mum were instantly nervous.

"I'm going to bed," Gran said, shooting another dark look at Granddad. "You don't need to panic."

Granddad sighed but did not speak.

"Shall I help you get to bed, Mum?" Dad asked.

"No thank you. I shall do it myself." Gran walked out of the room. "Goodnight all," she called, an unexpected spring in her step.

Lily decided to give Gran ten minutes to use the bathroom, then go to bed herself.

Waiting, she heard a soft click, like a door shutting. Then, swiftly after that, the wind knocked the branches of a tree against the window. A storm was coming.

After ten minutes of chat, Lily stood up.

"I'm off to bed," she said with a yawn.

"Good girl," Dad said.

Lily hugged everyone good night. Then she went into the hall, glancing at the front door to make sure it was shut. It was. Then, without noticing that Gran's new red scarf was no longer on the coat stand, she walked upstairs to bed. And Ernest's diaries.

SIXTEEN

France, 18 September 1918

Although I've only been here for a few weeks,
Fred, it's already hard to imagine any other world.
Sometimes we move on, chasing the Germans as
they retreat. Other times they dig in and resist.

Now, as I write, the enemy has the high ground
and is holding firm. Captain Whitaker believes
they've had reinforcements. More young soldiers
from the German cities, he says, fresh from school.
But they're not firing much. Captain Whitaker says
it's because they're rationing ammunition.

And so, at night, it's dead quiet. But it is not a peaceful quiet. It is a quiet that feels like a spring is coiled inside your chest. It's a deep, dark quiet, but that makes it worse. You know there will be noise, and that when it comes it will be horrific.

There're no clouds, and the stars stand out sharp in the cold sky. Ice crystals form on the top of our dugout.

It's not a time for sitting around. So I asked Captain Whitaker for permission to go out and reconnoitre the land ahead of us. I told him that the better I know the land, the better job I can do when he needs me.

"Did you do that with your races, Darby? Reconnaissance?"

"Yes, sir," I said. "I always did a recce to check the best routes, new landslips, the depth of streams, collapsed walls. My brother taught me the trick – of reading the landscape, remembering it, adjusting it. I'd move things – like lying flat stones under water – to make it easier for me on race day."

The memory hit me hard, Fred. How you used to take me on the race routes the night before and we'd check for the best lines.

The fells change season on season, year on year. Land slips and shifts. Walls are mended or collapse. Things that were there one year are not there the next.

I must have looked melancholy, and Captain Whitaker asked me about home.

"Tell me about where you live, Private Darby. I saw the village. But what's it like living there?"

I told him about the fells, the lake, the eagles and tarns, and how in autumn the paths become streams. About how the rain, when it comes hard, changes the face of a hillside.

"Do you know the Lakeland poets?" he asked. "Coleridge, Wordsworth?"

"A bit, sir," I replied. "I mean, we read them at school. Daffodils and all that. Did you?"

Captain Whitaker grinned. "I did," he enthused. "I do. I have a volume of Wordsworth in my pack. I suppose if you live there – if you know the fells – you don't need the poems?"

I shrugged. And we listened to a couple of shots fire off in the distance.

Captain Whitaker filled the silence. "I'd have liked to have met your brother," he said.

"I'd have liked that too, sir," I replied. "After the war ..." I stopped myself.

"After the war?" he prompted.

I frowned. "I was going to say you could come to our village and meet him."

Captain Whitaker smiled at me. And I couldn't

help but smile too. Then we were both laughing.

That was when I understood what I was starting to feel about Captain Whitaker. A bit like the way I felt about you, Fred. He was an older and a better man than me. I had this vision of him being killed. And I didn't like how that made me feel.

So I spent more time out in no man's land trying not to like Captain Whitaker too much.

And trying not to think how I would feel if he were killed.

SEVENTEEN

Lily was puzzled by a sudden gap in Ernest's diaries.
The next entry was November. Seven weeks later
than the last. She leafed back through the journal.
There were no pages missing. It was as if Ernest had
stopped writing for seven weeks.

But why?

Why would he do that?

Her first thought was that Captain Whitaker
had been killed, like Ernest had worried. But she
didn't really believe that could happen. This was a
diary, not a storybook.

France, 8 November 1918

We've been advancing across the open countryside. No more supply trenches and great fields of mud. We're now pushing on through fields and alongside hedges and fences. The land reminds me a bit of home. It's nice rolling countryside, but it's not like Cumbria. It's tame, no wilderness. Except for the bullets and shells, tanks and aeroplanes.

We've had rain for weeks, Fred. That's why I've not been able to write. Driving, soaking rain like the rain back home. No piece of paper would last a minute amid this downpour. It's even heavier tonight, but I'm under cover for once.

It's a quiet night. The Germans have been as good as gold. If they're still there. Some of the lads say they've all gone home, but for a handful of machine gunners. Other lads say the war isn't long *off ending. And, I'll admit, that brings mixed feelings.*

Who doesn't want this war to be over? Anyone would be mad to want it to go on. But for me, it's a problem. I am still doing this for you, Fred. I still want revenge for your death. If Captain Whitaker hadn't singled me out as a runner, I'd have seen a lot more action and a lot more Germans. Not that I blame the man.

He's given me ample opportunities to get out into no man's land. Every night, I run out to craters where our chaps are keeping an eye on the enemy.

I run out and take reports from them. Then run back to Captain Whitaker. I actually quite enjoy it. I'm fit, damn fit. If someone held a fell race tomorrow, I'd fancy my chances. But I'd be a bit weak on the hills – the only hill round here is infested with the enemy's machine-gun posts. You have to train for hills, as you knew.

Anyway, I was sat there, all those thoughts running through my head, the only one awake in the bottom of the trench, when Captain Whitaker comes over.

"Private Darby?" he said.

"Yes, sir," I answered. I jumped to my feet, assuming he had a run for me.

"I've not seen you writing for a while," he said. "And over the weeks it's something I've come to expect of you. Is everything all right? Have you run out of notepads?"

I laughed. "Too wet, sir. I'm a fair-weather writer, me."

He studied me, his eye twitching again. The water dripped off my helmet and onto my jacket, pooling on my trousers. I'd wedged my boots in a funk hole to keep them dry.

"Go into my bunker," Captain Whitaker offered.

"I'll take your post out here for an hour or so. Make yourself a cup of tea. In fact, I'll make it, then come back out."

"Thank you, sir," I said, and I followed Captain Whitaker into the bunker. Not much of a bunker, really. It was more like an extra width of trench dug into the side. There were a few wooden planks and some sort of material over the top, held in place by two thick beams on the end. But it was under cover. Captain Whitaker sat on a stool, pulled a map off his makeshift table and a ledger of some sort. I spotted a pile of three books by his bunk.

"Do you mind me asking, Darby?" the Captain started to say. "What is it you write? I've seen you at it for months – up until the last few weeks anyway. I think you're the only writer in my company. There's a few other poets up the line, but I don't think many can be as prolific as you. You must have gone *through half a dozen notebooks since you've been my runner."*

"I don't write poetry, sir. It's a diary, a long letter," I stumbled.

"But it's good to see you writing," he persisted. "Is it something you've thought of doing when this is all over?"

"Sir?"

"Writing." He looked serious. "I don't know. What do writers write? Stories? Poetry? Maybe a novel?"

I shook my head. "No, sir. I'm not a writer. I'm a farmer, if anything. That's what I've been doing since the war started."

"But you write all the time." Captain Whitaker laughed. "Until recently."

"No," I insisted. "I'm not a writer. It's odd – I've never really said so, but it's for our Fred."

Captain Whitaker flushed. "I'm sorry, Darby.

130

Dear God, forgive me prying into your life like that. I'll shut up."

"Fred asked me to write it, sir," I told him.

"I don't understand," he said, cautious.

"When Fred left to go and fight, sir. He told me to keep a record of my running. He said that when he was away I could write it all down for him to read when ..."

I couldn't find the words.

"When he came home after the war?" Captain Whitaker finished my sentence in a low voice.

I nodded, not able to speak.

"Forgive me for intruding," he said, leaning forward, clearly wanting to ask me more.

"It's fine, sir," I said, getting control of my emotions. "It started with me writing about my training, about what I ate and the races I did. But then I wrote more. About home, about the war. What

I read in the news. And I liked it. It made me feel ..." I hesitated. "It was like I could still talk to my brother, sir."

Captain Whitaker stood up. "Then I should go and cover your post, Darby," he said. "Leave you to talk to your brother. But I should say that is one of the finest, most human things I've heard since I've been out in this abattoir."

And then he left me to it, a frown fixed on his face. He pulled back the curtain and then he turned.

"It'll be over soon, Darby," he said, then went to join the other lads out in the rain.

Lily paused. She was supposed to be getting an early night, but she couldn't stop reading. She was coming to the end of the notebooks now. She had so many questions – her head was spinning with them. What happened next to Ernest? And Captain Whitaker? Did he survive? He'd made it this far. Lily recognised the date of the next diary entry: 11 November 1918. The last day of the First World War.

Armistice Day.

As Lily turned the pages of the notebooks, she sensed that her great-great grandfather was there with her, ready to tell her more.

EIGHTEEN

France, 11 November 1918

It's been a couple of days since I wrote, Fred. But it's not the rain that's stopped me. Not this time. We've been on the move. That's the thing. The Germans are in fast retreat, barely putting up a fight.

The main danger now isn't snipers and shellfire. It's the chaos the Germans leave behind – blowing up bridges, felling trees across roads and burning out all the roofs. So, as we advance, there's no cover from the rain. Nowhere to rest.

A couple of days ago, some of our lads entered

an old farmhouse with its roof still intact. And there, like a miracle, was a piano, immaculate and undamaged by shelling. One of the lads made a beeline for it, sat at the stool, cracked his fingers, then lifted the cover to reveal a set of perfect white and black keys.

He wouldn't have felt a thing.

Within a second, there was nothing left of him. There had been a booby-trap in the piano and now blood and rags of flesh sank into the dark soil around it.

Captain Whitaker is stretched to the limit. He takes every death as a personal catastrophe and incidents like that gnaw away at him. He has written too many letters home to mothers and fathers telling them what good soldiers their sons were and how proud they should be.

He called me over this morning. Six o'clock.

"*I need you to go back to HQ every day now, Private Darby. Maybe two or three times a day. To keep the lines open to and from Lieutenant Roberts and Major Evans. Understood?*" he asked.

"*Yes, sir,*" I replied.

"*We're near the end,*" he told me.

"*Yes, sir.*"

"*Do the men talk about it, Darby?*" he asked me suddenly.

"*About the end, sir?*"

He nodded.

"*They do. They're keen to end it, sir,*" I said.

"*But they don't want to just pack it in, sir,*" I went on, to be clear. "*All the men I speak to want to see it through. I mean, we're winning. We want the Germans to know they're defeated.*"

I ran freely back to HQ that morning, glad I'd told the

Captain where the men stood. There was no German artillery coming in. Few British sentries to worry about.

Just running. I shall relish the freedom of it when I get home to the fells.

The land I run over is no longer scattered with the debris of war. No rolls of wire. No lines of abandoned trenches. You see the odd abandoned vehicle or signs of a camp or a burned-out building. But it comes as a shock when you see things like that now. And for me, the greatest shock was a crashed aeroplane. I could see the French tricolour on the underside of the bottom wing. There was no body, but ivy was growing up the aeroplane and it was sinking into ground that had been flooded by the Germans. It looked as if nature was dragging it down, forbidding it to fly again. It made me wonder if that's what will happen after the war. If all the dead horses and men will be taken into the soil and turned over by ploughs in decades to come. Then I thought of you, Fred. That Mother said she would never have you back to bury. Your body. Where is it? Where are you?

I reached HQ around 0730 hours.

I could sense something was up. I could hear singing. Like they'd all gone mad.

"Runner from Captain Whitaker," I reported to the Major. "Captain Whitaker requesting information and permission to push on, sir."

The Major looked up at me. He was seated, his feet up on an ammunition box. At first I assumed he was injured, but there was no sign of bandages.

"Permission denied, Private," the Major said, lifting a tin cup to his lips. "Report back to Captain Whitaker and inform him of the following: 'Hostilities will cease at 1100 hours today, 11 November. Troops

will stand fast on the line reached at that hour.
There will be no intercourse of any description with
the enemy. Further instructions will follow.'"

"Sir?" I asked, unsure of what he meant.

"It's over, Private." The Major grinned. Then he
passed me his mug. "Finish this, son. And here's to
your health."

With whisky scorching my throat, I ran like
the blazes back to my company. I abandoned all
my usual care and – for the first time out there in
France – it felt like a real run, a fell race even. I gave
it everything, full-lunged, feeling the pain pouring
into my legs, because I was desperate to tell Captain
Whitaker the news. I knew he was teetering on the
brink, which meant that another week of this damn
war and his nerves would be shredded, but this news
would set him on the road to recovery.

Out there, in the abandoned fields and trenches,

I could tell that most men knew the war was over. The Armistice had been signed. There was no relentless barrage now and the skies, which had thronged with planes all autumn, were empty and quiet.

A few shells were still landing on either side. A whooshing great sound, the ground jumping, then the deafening boom of the explosion.

But even these seemed more like a gun salute from one army to another than the waging of war.

I came to a smashed-up village – ruins that used to be the homes of six or seven families. All I had ahead of me was this smooth field between me and Captain Whitaker and the other men, a few shoots of green like a haze on the soil's surface. A small chapel still stood, as if it was the one place in the whole of mainland Europe that hadn't been smashed or burned or witnessed pain and death. It looked like the kind of place where people would come now the war was over, to live and laugh and farm again.

I smiled.

Then, on the far side of the fields, I saw the sudden jump of the land, the sudden scatter of tonnes of earth into the air. Seconds later, I heard the dull thud of the shell.

I stopped and squatted, calculating what was to the left and right, so I knew where the shell had hit. Somewhere I would have been in five or ten minutes' time.

I had no doubts. It was a direct hit on Captain Whitaker's position.

NINETEEN

Lily was gripped. What now? What was going to happen to Captain Whitaker?

Was he dead?

Her great-great grandfather's story was as bleak and sad as any classroom read at school. As she stared at the log book, she heard raindrops hitting her bedroom window. They'd predicted a storm on the news. It meant the race route would be wet tomorrow. Harder going. But better for her.

Just as Lily was about to turn the page and find out Captain Whitaker's fate, she heard voices in the hallway outside her room.

142

Granddad. Then Mum.

Then she heard Dad say, "She'll be in with Lily."

Lily's door burst open.

"Where's Mum?" Dad asked, his eyes flitting wildly around the room.

Lily stood up. "I thought she was next door. In bed."

Dad shook his head. Behind him, in the hallway, Lily saw Granddad. His face was red, his hands held up to his mouth.

"She's gone," he moaned.

Downstairs, they found Gran's coat. But her boots and the red scarf Lily had bought for her had gone. It was quite clear what had happened. For whatever reason, Gran had gone out in the storm. Without a coat and as the night was coming down.

They organised themselves quickly. Granddad took Lily and Dad down to the village. They searched every shop and pub and restaurant. Nothing. Mum and Tim went from house to house to ask the neighbours. But none of them had seen Gran.

By the time the village had been searched, several people had gathered, offering to help. The police had arrived. A squad car, lights flashing. It was late now. An hour of daylight left at most. Lily knew that if they didn't find Gran in the next hour, they might never find her. She could read it in the faces of the adults. She had never seen expressions so serious.

Lily felt herself beginning to panic. Gran was missing. She wasn't wearing a coat. It was cold and raining harder now. The clouds to the west were black.

"We'll find her," Dad said to Lily, putting his arm round her. "The police are here. Mountain rescue are on their way."

"The fells." Lily gasped. "What if Gran is up there?"

"She won't be. She's not been up there for years," Dad said.

"So why are mountain rescue coming?" Lily asked.

Dad shrugged.

"I'm going up," Lily said.

"No," Dad said. "You mustn't."

"Why not, Dad? I'll find her if she's there."

Dad shrugged and Lily thought again how adults didn't always know what to do.

"I don't know," he said at last.

"I'll go," Lily said. "I promise to be back down before it gets really dark. OK?"

Dad closed his eyes. "OK," he said. "Go. But be careful."

Lily turned and ran. Up through the village

and onto the track that led up to the mines, then
the hill. She scanned left and right as she went,
breathing hard but stopping every minute to call out,
"Graaaaaaan."

No reply.

She met three pairs of walkers coming off the
hills, hoods up, flinching from the storm. Had they
seen an old woman walking around here? None of
them had, but they all offered to help the search.

Lily ran on, pushing herself. The skies grew
ever darker. Around her the sheep called out like
they always do at nightfall. Lily heard the scream
of a curlew. But in the back of her mind she was
thinking, *What if I set Gran off? What if she came on
the fells because of me talking about running? What
if it's my fault?*

But Lily knew it wasn't the time for self-pity – it
was time to rescue Gran. She ran on up to the mines,

where the fell opens up so you can gaze down at the lake. Lily scanned the fell, looking for movement or colour amid the grass and rock. But she couldn't see much – everything was blurring as the light diminished. Night was moving in like a curtain being drawn on the day. She had to go down. She had promised her dad.

Lily felt tears prickle in her eyes.

Maybe she should break that promise. Go higher and look down at the foot of the fell from above. Lily turned and sprinted hard. It was steep and rough. But she knew how to run, even though her clothes were heavy and wet, like those her great-great granddad had worn to run in during the war. And from deep inside she found power she'd never had before. A strength to tackle the hill. She ran until her lungs felt like they would explode, until she fell, cutting her palms on sharp rock as she vomited on the grass.

Lily breathed in deeply, then turned to look down the fell.

A flash of red. Red amid the greens and yellows and browns.

Lily shouted. Saw the red flash move. A hundred metres below her.

She felt an explosion of adrenaline.

"I'm coming, Gran," Lily screamed, then launched herself down the hill.

Fall down the hill. Fred's advice to Ernest. *Relax.*

Lily heard it and took long strides, checking only one footfall ahead as she bounded down off the scree and into the grass, along a pitted sheep track. She could see her gran, sitting down, staring at something in her hands. Mud. Her hands were filthy.

Lily slowed. Called softly, "Gran."

Gran looked up and smiled. "Lily," she said. "Take me home, love."

*

Mountain rescue came to meet them as they walked down past the mines. They had a blanket for Gran and another for Lily. Torches lit their way to a Land Rover, which drove Lily and Gran into the centre of the village. Lily saw Granddad in the crowd that had gathered. He was pushing people twice his size and half his age out of the way as he clamoured to reach his wife.

"Where did you go?" he said.

"Lily found me," Gran said, looking puzzled to be the centre of attention. "I knew she would."

As she walked back through the village, following the Land Rover, Lily saw Abbie and her dad standing in front of the village pub. Lily waved, but Abbie didn't see her, because she was looking at her dad, who was giving her one of his lectures.

"Where have you been?" he demanded.

"Searching," Abbie said. "I wanted to help."

"But where did you go?" he asked.

"Out on the fells."

"For God's sake, Abbie, you've got the race tomorrow. I told you not to. You need to conserve your energy."

"For God's sake, *Dad*." Abbie was shouting, her voice crackling with fury. "An old lady went missing. She was lost – alone in the dark and rain. They've found her now, but she could have died. Isn't that more important than a *race*?"

TWENTY

Once Gran was in bed and all the lights in the house were off, Lily had intended to get a good night's sleep, ready for the race.

But the wind and rain were wuthering against the window. And Lily couldn't stop thinking about Captain Whitaker. Had the shell killed him? She had to know.

France, 11 November 1918 (continued)

Something possessed me when I heard that shell come in and saw it hit our position. I set off hard, my mind scrambled. I had this vision of Captain Whitaker's bunker, his books knocked over, but your body under it all, Fred, not his, face down in the dirt, and, although I couldn't hear the shells coming in, I could feel the ground vibrating like it always did.

It was like running on a landslide. But the idea of stopping or changing direction didn't occur to me. One thought was overwhelming my mind. A promise. One of those promises you used to make. The promises that can't be broken. If I can have A, then I'll give up B.

You know.

So I swore, as I ran, that if Captain Whitaker could be spared, I would never run on the fells again, never race, never run anywhere. It was the most valuable thing I could think to give up, Fred. I scrambled and I ran and then I got there. The bunker.

Someone was shouting. No, not shouting. They were screaming out like an animal in the night.

As I dropped into the collapsed trench, now a mess of burst sandbags and shattered timber, I saw Captain Whitaker. He was leaning over a man, winding cloth around his upper arm. There was blood everywhere – it was pulsing out of the man like water out of a hole in a dam.

But Captain Whitaker was alive. My promise had saved him.

"In there," he shouted at me. "Corporal Wood. He's in the bunker."

I didn't need telling twice.

But I had to pass on the message first. That was my duty.

"Hostilities will cease at 1100 hours today, 11 November, sir," I reported, breathing in smoke and dust. "Troops will stand fast on the line reached at that hour. There will be no intercourse of any description with the enemy. Further instructions will follow."

"What?"

"Eleven. A ceasefire, sir. The Armistice was signed at five."

Captain Whitaker nodded. A slight hesitation, his mind taking it in before he went back to the there and then. Back to saving the injured man, because if we didn't, the Armistice would mean nothing to him and a lot less to us.

"Understood, Private Darby," he said. "Thank you. Now attend to Corporal Wood."

There was no light in the entrance of the bunker. Just smoke. And a smell that chilled me. I saw

Corporal Wood at the far end of the bunker, caught in a shaft of light from a gaping hole in the ceiling. The walls of the bunker dripped with flesh and bone. His flesh and bone.

Corporal Wood was dead. But his eyes were staring wildly at me. And, Fred, all I could think was that this was what you would have looked like when the shell hit you.

I kneeled down and closed his eyelids.

Then I touched his cheek and his back, his uniform stripped away by the blast. His skin was warm, Fred. Warm like when we used to share a bed in winter because it was so damn freezing, stealing each other's heat.

"Darby? Darby?" Captain Whitaker's voice was loud and rasping. Not how he normally called me.

I went to him.

The man he'd been tending to was smiling. He

had a big tin mug held up to his lips and I reckoned it was full of rum. His hand was bandaged up, but the bandage was crimson.

"This man's a runner, Darby," said the Captain. "Says there's a crater full of men north-west of here. Been there for two days, pinned down within range of two German machine-gun nests. Hit by a shell. Most of them injured. No water. No food. Desperate. Says they sent him for help."

"Sir?"

Captain Whitaker cleared his throat. "They've said if we don't get support to them by 1100 hours, they're going to storm the machine guns. They've a handful of Mills bombs, five working rifles and a pistol. The enemy will have been told to hold their line until 1100 hours, like we have. The Germans will have no choice but to engage our men."

"They'll be slaughtered, sir," I said.

"Indeed. And in the light of what you've just told me ... we're at the end, Darby. We need to stop their attack."

"I'll go, sir."

"Good man, Darby," Captain Whitaker said. "But be careful. Remember you promised to show me Cumbria?"

I nodded, then smiled at the other men. And not one of them smiled back. Their anxious faces looked at me. They knew this was the last order of the war. But they worried that, even though hostilities were about to finish, about to come to a longed-for end, the Great War could still play one last vicious trick on us.

On me.

TWENTY-ONE

France, 11 November 1918

My last mission of the war. Fifteen minutes. That's all I had. To stop six Tommies going over the top, all guns blazing, in the most futile act of the whole damn war. If I was late, if I didn't get to them by eleven, they might attack, desperate, not knowing they could just walk over to the German lines and shake hands with the enemy.

Time was running out.

I knew the crater I was heading for was under the escarpment the Germans had been holding. The other runner had described a shattered wood to the left. I knew to triangulate that with a half-smashed church tower to the right.

I saw it all in front of me. I was nearly there.

I took it steady when I came under the shadow of the escarpment. I'd been running in fine wintry sun at first, but the sun hadn't made it over the top of the hill where the Germans had their positions.

Shadow was good. I'd be less visible, filthy amid the mud. Any sniper or machine-gunner would struggle to hit me with the brighter light in the muddy fields behind me.

But would they shoot me, I wondered as I pushed on, determined not to fail these desperate men in this last hour of the war.

"Identify yourself."

It was a tired shout. But I knew to stick to protocol.

I stopped. Hands up. Then called back, "Private Darby, Border Regiment. With a message from Captain Whitaker."

A tin hat appeared with a gaunt grey face beneath it.

"Get down, man," the voice was louder now. "You're in their range of fire."

I scrambled down on my backside to see six men in the bunker, four of them with their heads or their arms bandaged up. One was unconscious, a messy wound on his leg exposed to the air. A pile of rifles dry on sacking between them. Then the smell reached me. The disgusting smell of the man's wound. It made me want to throw up. I could smell his flesh dying on his bones.

Five sets of eyes were on me. A wildness about them all.

I took a breath. "Captain Whitaker asks me to

inform you that the ceasefire begins at 1100 hours this morning."

Silence.

Five faces looked at me like I was a fool. Then one man stepped forward. I saw from his badge that he was a corporal. He looked at me blankly, a hint of a smile on his mud- and blood-crusted face.

"Ceasefire, Corporal," I repeated. "The Armistice was agreed this morning. There will be stretcher-bearers and supplies with you by midday. Your orders are to stay put."

I don't know what sort of reaction I expected from these men who were all set to fling themselves at death.

Maybe cheers and laughter? Did I expect that?

Instead, they turned to each other, and to me, and shared silent grim handshakes. Then one of them fell back against the side of the crater and sobbed.

The Corporal put his filthy hand on the man's shoulder and stared out across the mud.

I was about to head back to confirm to Captain Whitaker that I had reached the men – and to update him on their condition – when there was the whoosh of a shell coming over. It hit the open land I'd come across. We watched the earth jump, then heard the thud.

"Emptying their guns," the Corporal mused. "You be careful out there, son."

"I will, sir," I said.

Then I was off again for another run across the battlefields. I moved at a steady pace. My whole body was suddenly very tired. And, in my head, a question hummed. Well, two questions. One followed on from the logic of the other.

The first question was: what now? What would happen next? Would we pack up and go home and I could say I'd done my duty?

Then the follow-on question: had I done my duty? What had my duty been?

To my country, my duty was to fight, yes. But the reason I'd come to fight was to avenge you, Fred. And I hadn't. I'd not taken a German life.

Suddenly – with the war over – that seemed vital. How could I walk the roads of our town, past the places of our childhoods, the rope swing, the lake, the steamer and always feel I'd not done right by you?

But I also knew that was wrong. Our father and mother would have told me it was wrong. To want to take a life just so I could live with myself. My mind was confused. I couldn't think straight.

These were my thoughts as I ran from what I thought would be my last critical action of war. What I didn't know was that there was more to come.

TWENTY-TWO

France, 11 November 1918 (continued)

The first shell came in like a train rocketing past when you're standing on a platform. Full steam ahead, knocking you over as it carves its way through the air.

I was lifted off my feet when it hit. My nose full of the sharp pain of explosives. I could taste blood in my mouth. My ears buzzed like my head was in a beehive.

Covered in soil, I scrambled back to my feet.

Like the Corporal had said, the Germans were emptying their guns into what they thought were empty fields.

I knew I had to get out of there. To safety. I'd been lucky so far. But who knew how many more unspent shells the Germans wanted to get rid of? And maybe the British and French would join in too.

I thought back to the maps I'd studied and remembered there was a village a mile to the north. I'd run to the village. There, I would be safe.

When I got there, my first thought was that the village was empty. The streets weren't really streets. They were more like canyons of rock, with barricades at the far end. What used to be a town hall, houses and cafes were smashed, pouring rubble into the streets. It was like one of those crevasses we used to run up, Fred. Rock on either side and more rock strewn across the ground.

Charred wood stuck out where floors used to be. There were clothes strewn around and smashed plates, a bed. On the left a building that was *completely intact. It stood out, as if it had been built after the bombing. It seemed impossible it could be standing at all.*

Thick grey dust covered everything.

I tried to imagine our village like this. The butcher's, the pub, the boat house, our house – all smashed to pieces. That was the only way I could imagine what this used to be.

In the distance, I thought I could hear bells ringing, like the church bell calling people to worship. Then I saw a huddle of people cowering in the open.

This was their town. They were the people of the town. But they looked more like vagrants in a strange city.

Their eyes were wild, just like the six soldiers I'd left. They were eyes that have seen too much.

A man stood up and walked two paces towards me, blocking my view of the others, but I'd seen some children, women. And then a bedraggled figure on his knees beyond them, head down, next to a brazier, flames leaping from it into the sky.

"English?" the man called to me.

I held my arms out, clear of my rifle over my shoulder.

"English," I told him.

He looked nervy. Nervy like he would do something, anything, to protect his people. He was wearing old filthy clothes, but still he had a silk scarf tied in a perfect knot at his neck.

Then he fired a volley of questions at me.

"What is happening? Why are you here? Where are the French army? Why has the noise stopped? Are they all dead?"

"La guerre est finie," I interrupted. "Guerre," I said again, clearly. "Finie."

For a few seconds, there was silence. Then the

man burst out laughing, flung his arms out and lunged at me.

As he held on to me, in a tight grip that squeezed the air from my lungs, he was joined by others. People emerged from the cellars around us. Four children and two young women. And one older woman, about Mother's age, stood further back, eyes dark and serious, staring deep into me, and I could not look away until she did.

Then a very old man approached, walking slowly, raising his stick to me in greeting as I stared back at the one figure who had not come to greet me.

I saw that he was a young man, even younger than me. He was still kneeling, dirty and tired, but clearly no older than seventeen. His grey uniform was torn, worn to threads. He had no boots on. He was covered not in wounds but red blotches that I knew meant he was infested with lice.

And then I noticed his hands bound behind his back.

I stepped back from my host.

"Le garçon?" I asked. Then corrected myself. "Soldat?"

"Soldat." The man nodded, as if to reinforce my correction, then said, "Execution." He waved his arms to take in the ruin of his village. The row of three graves with crosses in what looked like an old garden.

I understood.

I shook my head. I couldn't let that happen. I couldn't allow these French villagers to kill this German soldier, this boy. They were civilians. They would have to live with their actions after the war. Better they had grief and loss and rage to deal with. They didn't need guilt and remorse as well. Imagine going back to normal life in this town, when this square was rebuilt. *Shopping for bread. Waving to a friend. Talking to a neighbour over coffee. Going to church. All in the place where they'd killed a boy.*

Execution of the enemy was not a job for a civilian. It was a job for a soldier.

TWENTY-THREE

France, 11 November 1918 (continued)

"It is my duty to arrest him," I informed the Frenchman who had embraced me. "I am a soldier. He is an enemy soldier. I must take him as a prisoner. These are my orders."

"You don't always have to follow orders." He smiled.

"I do," I replied.

His answer was a shrug, and there was a look in the Frenchman's eyes, like he knew I wanted to take this German and kill him.

"Il est un garçon," *I added.* "La guerre est finie à onze heures. Oui?"

"Oui." *The man threw his arms in the air.*

Then the woman with the intense stare, who had not taken her eyes off me since I arrived, stepped forward. She spoke in perfect English, posh English, but her teeth were bared. As she spoke, explosions boomed in the background.

"I have lost all three sons to this war," *she said in a rasping voice. Then she grabbed the German boy by the shredded material of his sleeve. He tried to pull away, but he was panting like a dog and she had his jacket in a tight grip.*

"I'm sorry," *I said.*

"And, when you say the war finished at eleven, I disagree," *she stated.* "For me, the war will never end. Every moment of my life I will live with this war in my head and my heart."

"I'm sorry," I said again.

"Do not be sorry for me," she went on. "It is not your fault. You, the British, have not killed my sons. The Germans did. Germans in uniforms like this." She ripped the boy's sleeves down to his hands. Then she gripped his arm with both her hands. You could see his flesh white between her fingers.

"Give him to me," she demanded.

"No," I said. "It is my duty—"

The woman pulled the young soldier off his knees.

"Walk away," she told me. "No one will care what happens to another German. A million dead. Or a million and one. What does one man matter?"

I looked into her eyes and I understood. She wanted revenge. She wanted his death to make up for her three sons. Just like I wanted revenge for you, Fred.

"He is a boy," I said. "Not a man."

"My boys were boys," she came back at me. "Now they will never be men."

I didn't know what to say to that. Dust and fire and smoke mingled in the air, forcing me to cover my mouth.

"Who does one last soldier matter to?" she said again, her voice rasping as her anger rose.

I heard myself say it before I thought it.

"His mother?" I suggested.

She stepped back like I'd slapped her.

And in that moment, none of the others intervened. They all avoided my eyes. But she was still eyeing me, the tight rage of her face collapsing.

"D 'accord," she muttered.

I walked out of the village, the German boy in front of me. I carried my rifle, the bayonet pointed at him.

I could see he was trying to walk proudly, but I could also tell he expected me to shoot him.

He was still panting, but I knew it wasn't fear. It was thirst. He'd probably not had a drink for hours. Or days. But I only had a little water. And it was my water.

"What is your name?" I asked.

"Thomas," he replied.

The guns had stopped firing. No shells. No machine guns. I could hear water running somewhere. A river? I could hear the wind in what was left of the trees that lined the road.

"How old are you?" I asked.

"Twenty."

"No. How old are you really?" I asked again.

He stopped.

"Sixteen," he admitted, too scared to look me in the eye.

"Where are you from?" I asked, swallowing my shock that a child his age, a couple of years younger than me, should be anywhere near these fields of war.

"München," he replied. Then he asked his own question. "Where are you from?"

"Cumbria, England," I said. "The Lake District."

Then he said a word I didn't catch. Well, I wasn't sure I heard it right.

"What did you say?" I asked. "I didn't understand."

"Wordsworth," he said, and walked on.

I stopped him, then cursed and handed him my water.

"Drink this," I said.

I could never have killed him, Fred.

TWENTY-FOUR

Gran was sitting at the table when Lily walked into the kitchen. In front of her was a plate with two slices of toast, a small pile of postcards tied together with brown string, and Ernest's fell-running medals. The postcards were scattered with crumbs.

"Hi, Gran," Lily said, nervous about how she would be this morning.

Gran smiled. "I think I have something to thank you for, don't I?"

A wave of emotion washed over Lily. She could feel her bottom lip wobble. *I'm going to cry*, she said to herself. *Don't cry in front of Gran.*

But it was no good. She was crying.

Gran put her toast down and held her arms out. She said nothing and Lily went to her and let herself be hugged. Gran gave the best hugs, her old strong arms circling her. Lily closed her eyes and felt a deep-down happiness she'd not felt all weekend.

"So, today's your big day, Lily," Gran said, releasing her.

"I suppose." Lily rubbed her face. The race had barely registered after last night on the fells. Losing Gran, then finding her. Reading Ernest's diary to the end. This hug. Family. That's what was really important.

"Shall I come and watch?" Gran asked.

"Yes, please."

Gran took another bite of her toast, then studied it for a moment before she asked, "Did you find out?"

"Find out what?" Lily started, immediately on her guard.

"Why Ernest gave up running," Gran said.

Lily wasn't sure what to say at first. She could lie and say she had no idea. She could change the subject. But neither option felt right. Her gran was old and could become confused. But not all the time. Sometimes she was just like she'd always been. Lily owed her the truth.

"I did," Lily said.

"And?" Gran leaned forward.

Lily swallowed, hoping she was doing the right thing.

"Ernest made a promise," she began. "When he was in the war. It was right at the end and a shell fell near his friend – Captain Whitaker. Ernest promised himself that if his friend survived, he would never run again. It was like a prayer. Or a wish." Lily paused. "And it came true."

Gran smiled, as if she was pleased by the story. "We never knew," she said.

"I think it's nice." Lily tried to think of the right word. "Honourable."

"It is very nice," Gran said. "It shows he was willing to give up what he loved to save a friend."

"And that he kept his promises," Lily added, her heart swelling with emotion because Gran was Gran, back to her best. Kind. Thoughtful. Lovely.

"That's true," Gran nodded, then picked up one of the postcards in front of her.

Lily watched her as she studied it, turning it over in her hand. Her gran's hand was wrinkled and a bit crooked, but Lily had always liked that about her. And she liked the smell of her gran's kitchen too. A sort of toasty marmalady smell.

"Was Captain Whitaker's first name Thomas?" Gran asked, looking at Lily.

"I don't remember," Lily said. "Why?"

Gran pushed the pile of postcards towards Lily.

"I've had these. For years. I remembered them last night – after our little adventure on the fells."

Lily walked over to stand next to Gran and lifted the first one off the top. Of all the postcards it was the one that had been handled the most. It was papery, the card not as stiff as the others. She read:

Dear Ernest

Greetings from München. We have beautiful weather. And I have beautiful news also. I am a father. Our son was born one day ago. He is strong and lean and has wide-open eyes. His name is Ernest. Send me a postcard soon, my friend.

Thomas

Lily put her hand to her mouth.

"What is it, love?" Gran asked.

"Thomas was a German soldier," Lily said. "Ernest – well, Ernest sort of saved his life."

Then Lily sat down and told her gran the story of Ernest and Thomas.

Enemies for an hour, who became life-long friends.

TWENTY-FIVE

Lily pushed herself to the front for the start of the race. It was something she never usually did, but today she would. They were all at the lakeside, where the junior races started. They would run through the village, hard up the hill, then down again.

She stared up the fell. It meant more to her than ever now. It was the fell where she'd found her gran. The fell where Ernest won his race. She wondered how many stories one mountain could tell. She checked her bum bag. The race rules were that you carried a waterproof jacket. That was it. But Lily had something else in her bum bag. A small cloth bag tied with string at the top. In it was Ernest's winner's medal. Her gran had insisted she take it – and keep it. Lily wanted another medal to add to it. The thought gave her a surge of adrenaline that swept away all the tiredness and stress of the last few hours.

She was ready.

The sun shone down from the far end of the lake and made the water glitter. But Lily was glad that the air was still cool. Abbie was there but, as usual, her dad had kept her away from the other runners, waving his finger at her, pointing up the hill. Lily had seen her stumble away from him to be sick.

"Four minutes yet, girls," the race organiser called.

Lily stood with the others, staring up the hill. It was hard not to think about what she had read last night. And about Gran and what had happened to her. But this was a race. A race was a chance to forget all the stuff in her head – the good and the bad. It was a chance to run. And where better to run and celebrate what her great-great grandfather had done – and what he had not done – than here on his fell?

Lily grinned.

She stood firm on the front row, making her body rigid so the girls pushing behind could not move her. She refused to look at them or take part in the jostling. She just stared up at the fell and traced the paths she imagined Ernest would have run on his race.

Lily wished the race today wasn't an under-15s race but an adult race. She longed to run beyond the initial slopes, pick her way among the gullies and rocks to the top. Run beside the tarn that Ernest had mentioned in his log book.

She stared at the hill and a smile broke out on her face. The sun was out, touching the very tops of the fells. The water of the lake was rippling behind her. And she could hear the murmur of the families who had come to watch the fell race.

"Two minutes," said the organiser.

Lily held her ground but glanced left down the lake to an old gnarled tree. The rope swing dangled over the water, shifting in the breeze. She smiled.

"One minute, girls."

Lily stood tall. She breathed in deeply. *No more thoughts about last night*, she said to herself. It was time to race. She could think later.

Lily slapped her thighs hard, then glanced at Abbie, who was alone, two metres down the line. Her face looked pale and puffy.

Their eyes met.

"Good luck," Lily said.

"You too." Abbie tried to smile, but it was tense, forced.

"Look," Lily said, "I saw you helped to search for my gran last night. Thank you."

"That was your gran?" Abbie said. "I didn't know. Is she OK?"

"Fine. A bit shaken. But I mean it, Abbie. Thanks."

"Any time." Abbie grinned, a real grin this time.

Both girls looked at the line scored into the earth at their feet.

"GO!"

Lily pushed off hard, pumping her arms fast, moving left to the inside of the bend in the track, one of the first group of six or seven runners. They all moved right as the track bent back the other way. Then the hills began to rise, steady at first. As she ran, Lily pushed concerns about Abbie and how far behind she was out of her mind and replaced them with Ernest.

Ernest running through no man's land.

Ernest running through the carnage of war to save a desperate group of soldiers.

Ernest's anger about Fred. Ernest wanting revenge.

Attack the hill. Attack it.

Fourth.

Third.

Second.

No sign of Abbie.

Then, with a huge effort, imagining Ernest powering along beside her, Lily forced herself past a tall girl in a striped vest.

First.

But Lily wasn't going to ease off now. There was over half a mile of uphill left, before the route swung right to come down a softer grassy descent. Lily had to cover that distance hard. She had to create enough of a gap between her and the other runners – and Abbie – so they couldn't tear past her on the way down.

Lily gave it everything. All the time she felt Ernest there with her, to her right, urging her on. She could almost see him out of the corner of her eye.

She allowed herself a look behind at the top as she turned. Five runners, Abbie leading them. The sight of her rival gave Lily another boost. She accelerated fast along a narrow footpath as the hill flattened out, gasping "Thank you" to the race marshal who stood at the turn.

Then another marshal.

Another gasped thank-you.

Down the hill.

Narrow path.

Grass at the edge.

Soil and roots.

Lily strode out, extending each stride, covering more ground, the foot strikes sending shockwaves up her legs. She remembered how she'd run down the hill last night to get to Gran, trying to do what Fred had told Ernest.

It was working.

She was striding out, watching the ground ahead of her. No time to look back. A mile to go.

Lily drove her feet harder into the ground.

"Come on, Lily," came a shout from the side of the fell. A man's voice, but whose? Not her dad's. She knew he was down at the finish with a bottle of water for her.

So who was it?

No time to think about that. Only the race. The

next four minutes. Still in the lead. Harder. Faster. More and more reckless. No sound of anyone behind her. Through a stream, sudden and cold, leaping the last bit to avoid the rocky bed.

Then – at last – footsteps behind her. One runner. Maybe two.

Four hundred metres to go.

Nearly there.

Back on the main tourist path. The track once used by miners. And by Ernest and his brother. By generations of runners on the magnificent fell.

A last slight uphill. No more than three hundred metres now as Lily felt Abbie push past her.

Always Abbie at the end.

But Lily wasn't going to give in this time. She was more than Lily today. She was Ernest Darby's great-great granddaughter. Ernest Darby, the legendary fell racer.

Lily pushed, counter-attacking, the two of them level now.

Neck and neck. Lily was sprinting like she'd never sprinted before.

One hundred metres to go.

Lily forced her legs and her lungs to keep their power and their pace. She pushed one, then two, then three metres ahead of Abbie.

Fifty metres to go.

Abbie was attacking again.

The wind was in Lily's hair. The sound of a storm raged in her ears.

Abbie was level. They were neck and neck again, their strides matched.

Twenty metres.

Lily saw the light of the lake glittering, the silhouettes of people in front of it. It was just like Ernest had described it. She looked into the light and saw the silhouette of a soldier, his uniform heavy on his body.

Lily took one last gasp and thrust herself forward.

Over the line.

A metre.

No more.

But she'd done it. Abbie was behind her. Lily had won!

Lily's legs buckled as she fell to her hands and knees, closed her eyes. She felt like she had just emerged from being buried under the fell, the weight of it on her chest only just released. She took great gasps of air as her stomach cramped, her whole body pulsing in agony.

"Are you OK, girls?" A race official's hand was on her shoulder, her voice calm amid the shouts of the crowd.

Lily nodded. Coughed. Breathed. Then she stood to walk in a circle. To make the pain in her legs go away.

But she couldn't even walk, so she sat down again, wanted to cry. And there was her dad, handing her water.

"Thanks," Lily gasped.

Dad stayed silent as she sipped her water, then poured some on her face. Then she glanced back at Abbie, who was on the ground, still retching.

Alone.

Abbie's dad was standing away from everyone, staring at the ground, his face set with anger. And Fred's phrase came to Lily. Not Ernest's.

If someone is troubled, be the first to comfort them. Then you can be proud of yourself.

Lily stood up and staggered towards Abbie.

She slumped down and handed her rival the water.

"Cheers." Abbie took a big grateful gulp. "Is that your gran?" she asked.

Lily looked over and saw her gran waving. "Yeah."

Lily waved back. Abbie too.

Gran clasped her two hands up together and moved them side to side like a boxer who's just won a fight.

Abbie nudged Lily and laughed. "I'm glad you won. See how proud your gran is of you."

"I know," Lily said, "and I'm proud of her."

"I'll just have to beat you next time."

"Maybe," Lily laughed.

THE FIRST WORLD WAR AND THE ARMISTICE

The First World War was a conflict on a scale the world had never seen before. It lasted over four years and it is estimated that over 18 million people died, soldiers and civilians, while over 23 million were wounded.

In 1918, when it became clear that they could not win the war, the Germans had to agree to the demands of the Allied leaders of Britain, France and the USA. The war ended with the signing of the Armistice, or peace agreement, in a railway carriage in the French forest of Compiègne. At 11 a.m. on 11 November 1918 – the eleventh hour of the eleventh day of the eleventh month – the guns finally fell silent.

The Armistice was signed early in the morning of 11 November. Most soldiers were told quickly by their officers, who had heard via radio, telephone and from runners, that hundreds of thousands of men on both sides would lay down their arms at the same time later that morning. But some were harder to reach, even using runners. As a result, there were several skirmishes and confused firing of shells and bullets even after 11 a.m., leading, sadly, to the deaths of even more young men.

For many, the war would never be over. The horrific things that they had seen would live on in their minds for ever. A whole generation of young men had been lost and their families left to grieve.

In most towns and villages in the UK, there are memorials to those who died. During my research, I have also visited the graveyards in France and Belgium. As you travel across what is now beautiful countryside, it seems there are endless cemeteries, each with hundreds or thousands of bodies laid to rest. The cemeteries are confusing places. On the one hand, you feel horrified by the number of perfectly tended graves; on the other, you are inspired by how they are remembered in this way over a century later.

The First World War was supposed to be the war to end all wars, but only twenty-one years later, after the rise of Hitler in Germany, the world would find itself caught up in another horrific conflict.

THE INSPIRATION FOR ARMISTICE RUNNER

When Tom is writing, he finds inspiration in lots of different places. Here are the ten things that inspired him to write *Armistice Runner*.

ONE

Tom likes fell running, which is running up and down hills and across moors mostly in the north of England. He's been doing it for a few years now and often competes in races, usually towards the back. He did finish 22nd in a race once, but that was because the first 50 runners went the wrong way and were disqualified.

TWO

Fell running has an amazing history. It originated when villages had their annual fair and those who were willing raced up and down the nearest hill or mountain to see who was fastest. Fell running is most popular in the north of England. There are several fell-running clubs in the UK. You can find out more at www.fellrunner.org.uk.

THREE

Tom's daughter likes to fell run too. She is much faster than her dad. A lot of *Armistice Runner* relates to children and teenagers fell racing. The storyline was inspired by Tom's daughter and the other runners she races with.

FOUR

Fell runners have to be able to run up and down sometimes steep hills and be ready to deal with a lot of mud. They recce routes just like Ernest does in this book, working out the best way to leap over stiles and the safest path through running water or a sodden moor.

FIVE

When the First World War broke out, many fell racers volunteered to fight. Tom read about them in history books and Ernest Dalzell in particular was a big inspiration to him. He was famous for insanely speedy descents and for cycling a hundred miles to get to and from a venue on race day. Sadly, Dalzell was killed in the war.

SIX

One race that Tom has run is the Burnsall Classic Fell Race, where Ernest Dalzell broke the record in 12 minutes and 59 seconds. That record stood for nearly seventy years.

Tom wanted to do the race to get into the mind of a man like Dalzell, although with a time of 26 minutes 35 seconds he didn't threaten the record. But he was still proud of himself.

SEVEN

Tom has written books about the First World War before: *Over the Line*, *The Last Try* and *Fly Boy*. While researching those books, Tom read about the Armistice and became fascinated by the last days of the war and how it was possible to stop everyone waging war all at exactly the same moment.

EIGHT

Tom read about the impact the First World War had on the Lake District communities. One account was about a man who refused to go to war and hid among the fells, living in shepherds' huts. This was one of the true stories Tom grafted into *Armistice Runner*.

NINE

When Tom was a boy, he visited the Lake District twice a year for camping holidays with his mum and dad. He came to love the fells and lakes, spending hours walking and canoeing.

Tom has continued to visit the Lake District with his wife and daughter, who both love it there too. Tom tries to arrange school visits in Cumbria as an excuse to go back as often as he can.

TEN

When Tom goes to First World War cemeteries, he always visits the German graves as well as the British and Commonwealth graves. Young men on both sides had little choice but to fight in the First World War. With this in mind, Tom wanted to end *Armistice Runner* with a friendship between a British and a German soldier.

Tom has created a webpage with lots of interesting extra information about *Armistice Runner*, including videos, blogs and quizzes, on his website:

www.tompalmer.co.uk/armistice-runner

You can also contact him there if you have any questions about this or any of his other books.

ACKNOWLEDGEMENTS

Every book I write depends on the help of a lot of people. *Armistice Runner* is no exception. But two people do stand out. One is my daughter. The other is Jane Walker at my publisher Barrington Stoke. Thank you to both, who, in different ways, showed great stamina to make this book possible.

Thank you also to my wife. And Ailsa Bathgate, Emma Hargrave and the fantastic team at Barrington Stoke. David, Rebecca and Nick at David Luxton Associates. I'd also like to thank the fell-running community who put on races for children and adults and make a day out on the fells and moors the best possible choice for a weekend – in snow, wind and sun.

Thank you, too, to Deborah Levens and her daughter and Jim Sells for reading and commenting on the book.

I read some great books as research for writing *Armistice Runner*. *Voices from the Past: Armistice 1918* by Paul Kendall and *Keswick in the Great War* by Ruth Mansergh helped with the history. And for fell running I turned to *Run Wild* by Boff Whalley, *Feet In the Clouds* by Richard Askwith and *It's a Hill, Get Over It* by Steve Chilton, in which I read about the legends of fell running, notably Ernest Dalzell, who broke the record for the Burnsall Fell Race not long before he went to fight in the First World War, where, sadly, he was killed.